DIARY OF AN OLD MAN

Chaim
Bermant

DIARY OF AN OLD MAN

Holt,
Rinehart and
Winston

New York Chicago
San Francisco

Designer: Ernst Reichl
80895–0317
Printed in the United States of America

In Memory of Aziel Boruch
Who Would Have Enjoyed Old Age
Had He Been Spared for It

DIARY OF AN OLD MAN

They buried old Harry this morning. I don't know why I call him old Harry, but old Harry it's been for as long as I've known him. He was 74—tried to make out he was only 73, but he was 74 if a day, and a nice old soul, but he didn't wear well. Some men don't begin to straighten out till they get widowed—as if the wife kept them from the sun; others fall apart. Harry was a faller-apart. He used to say; "It's all right for you, Cyril. You lost your Elsie when you were still a young man. You had time to get used to your own company. But Deirdre and me have been together for thirty-eight years. It's a bit late at my age to get used to myself." He went up to his bed straight after her funeral and never came down, at least not on his own legs.

I'd been kept indoors myself by my bad leg and the bad weather so that I hadn't seen him for over a week, and he was poorly then, sitting up with a

9

cardigan over his pajamas, and in woolen mittens, and shivering so hard that his teeth in the glass beside him chattered.

"I haven't long to go," he kept saying in a quiet voice.

"Nonsense," I said, "you're good for another twenty years."

"Another twenty years?" he said.

"At least."

At this he was silent for a bit, then he said: "You don't mean it, do you?"

"Why not? People live to all sorts of ages nowadays. Why only this morning I saw a fellow in hospital who was a hundred; they were having a party for him. He couldn't walk or see or hear, but he was a hundred."

At this he turned even whiter than he was and began crying. He must have died the next day or the day after. He'd been dead nearly a week when they found him. He had fallen out of bed and if it wasn't for his cat going mad with hunger and screeching the place down he might have lain there for months.

It was a small funeral. There was his sister Rachel, older than him by two years, who stood looking into the grave as if wishing she was there herself; a parson, a small man with a red face, blue ears, and adenoids; George, his friend and mine, and myself. There was no one else, except the gravestones, covering a whole hillside like spec-

10

tators at a terracing, and a flock of seagulls, some overhead, noisy and messy, some perched on the stones, listening respectfully, as if they were relatives.

Snow had fallen the day before, but it was melting on the tree-tops and the drops were peppering the snow on the ground. It was slightly foggy.

We walked home together, George and I, him sighing and me sighing and hardly a word between us, but then as we got to his place he suddenly turned to me and said, "There's only thee and me now—he had that odd way of speaking—"only thee and me, and I'm half gone."

I was going to say, "Nonsense, you're good for another twenty years," but remembered what happened when I said it to Harry.

And he went on, "Do you remember this time last year?"

"This time last year?"

"Yes, almost to the day."

"Almost to the day?"

"Yes, this time last year."

And then I remembered.

"Dick, poor old Dick."

"Yes," he said, "almost to the day, wasn't it?"

"It couldn't be that long ago though, could it?"

"A year ago almost to the day, the same parson, the same graveyard. Ah, but there was a crowd of us then. Albert, Stephen, Ernie, Bill, my elder brother Sam, Philip—"

11

"And old Harry."

"And old Harry. Half the town was there. Where are they now?"

"Gone."

"Every bleeding one of them, except thee and me."

"It's been a bad winter."

"It's not only that, Cyril. It's psychological. People have a habit of doing as their friends do."

"You mean keeping up with the Joneses?"

"Keeping down with the Joneses would be a better way of putting it. I mean it mightn't occur to them that they're thinking about it, but deep, deep down, so deep that there's no knowing it's there, they want to do as the rest of them. If you're part of a close group you don't want to be an outsider."

I stopped to think about this for a bit, then I said, "You didn't mean that because old Harry died you'd like to do the same, do you, George?"

"Of course not, at least not consciously. But there's the sub-conscious. You know what the sub-conscious is, don't you?"

"The part of the conscious that isn't."

"No, that's the unconscious. The sub-conscious is the part of the mind that thinks on the quiet. It has ideas of its own without you ever knowing it."

"Without you knowing it?"

"Yes. Then there's the super-conscious. It worries about things you'd like to forget about."

"Like bills and things?"

"Yes, things like that. Then there's the id."

"The yid?"

"The id—I-D—id, and the ego. All very complicated psychology, but if you don't know psychology you don't know what's happening to you."

"You don't, do you?"

"Not without psychology."

"No."

"There was the time when a fellow was well set-up in this world if he could read and write, but not today."

"No, not today."

"He'll get nowhere without psychology."

As long as George kept talking I could keep Harry from my mind, but as soon as he stopped he was almost there with us, with his big, white face and sad, gray, watery eyes.

It got very cold again toward night, and when I got back to my room I remembered that I had forgotten to mend my paraffin-stove. It was like a cellar, so cold that the air hit you like a wall. I lit the gas-stove and put the kettle on, but that didn't help much. The window frames were shaky so even with my heating full on the cold still came in.

I made myself a cup of tea, took off my overclothes, put on pajamas over my underclothes and a sweater over my pajamas, and a Balaclava helmet, and I was ready for bed.

13

A man's best friend is his bed, as long as he can get in and out as he wants. I had a little table by my bed where I kept my books and papers and the glass for my teeth. I had a wireless there too and a little tray for my tea. In fact, if it wasn't for my sewage problems, I had everything I needed in the world within arm's reach.

I had been feeling a little sorry for myself, trudging homewards through the slush, but now, sitting up in bed, I could count my blessings.

There was my room, big, with two windows and a fine view of the street. There was the earthenware cat on the mantelpiece. I had a sink and a gas-ring behind a fancy screen, though it was getting a bit less fancy because it had caught fire once or twice. The fireplace had been closed up with hardboard but I decorated it with a picture of Her Majesty the Queen wearing the Most Noble Order of the Garter. The ceiling was covered with fancy plaster, leaves, fruit, and whatnot, which sometimes came snowing down on top of me; but if I was too tired to do anything else I could lie on my back for hours and imagine the shapes do all sorts of things. I also have a big leather armchair stuffed with horsehair. The horsehair can be a bit ticklish if you've got a sensitive bottom, but George fancies it no end and plonks himself there with every chance he gets. In fact, I think there is something on between him and that chair, as I once caught him on it with his trousers off.

Then there's my wireless. I've had it for twenty-seven years, and I can no longer get any of the fancy stations like Radio Luxembourg, but the Home and Light come through loud and clear, and especially the Home, which is good enough for me. And it's mine, with everything paid for, even the license.

There's my friends, not many now, but the older a fellow gets the fewer he needs. I still have the Christmas cards they sent me on the mantelpiece, on either side of the earthenware cat, all robins and holly, one from George, one from Mrs. McConnachie—my landlady—and one from old Harry. Poor old Harry.

We were in the A.R.P. together, Harry and I. We didn't have much luck down our way, not as much as a bomb, and the nearest thing we had to action was when a workman pierced a gas main with a pneumatic drill, but we had fine times together, with whist and mugs of tea in the warden's post, and stories about the First World War. Not a patch on the first one, the second one. Harry was in Mespot, a corporal, and he came out with a whole row of gongs and bits of shrapnel all over the place, and also malaria which kept coming back to him as regular as bronchitis comes back to me. Never missed a Remembrance Parade for as long as I'd known him, except last November. When he missed that I knew all was over.

I suppose with his shrapnel, his malaria, and

his seventy-four years he had a right to die, but he had more to live for than any of us. He had a son and daughter whom he hadn't seen for years, but still they were there somewhere in the world, and he had a sister. And he had money too. They used to keep a sweet and tobacco shop and he retired with quite a bit. He had a comfortable house with television and he could switch on the heating and leave it on whenever he felt cold. Not that he did, for he was a bit tight, and I suppose I would be myself if I had anything to be tight with. People live to all sorts of fancy ages nowadays and you don't want your money to run out before you do.

Poor old Harry. I was sorry for him when he was ill in bed with his teeth chattering there beside him, and I didn't like the sight of him in the box, silent and nailed up, but when he was lowered into the ground, and the earth, brown with flecks of snow, was thrown on top of him; he seemed to become part of it. I suppose the older you get the more you become like soil.

It was getting dark now. There was snow on the sill and on the window frame. It was black with dust, but it had begun to melt a little. It was the middle of February. The warmer weather was on the way. Soon it would be spring and I would have walks in the park again, or sit on the bench outside and watch the traffic go by. The road takes a sharp turn near here and at the rush hour it's always good for a smash-up or two.

The door slammed downstairs and there came
a squelch of boots. Mrs. McConnachie was back
from work. It must be twenty to five, I thought.
I looked at my watch, though I needn't have done,
for twenty to five it was.

Mrs. M, as I said, is my landlady, and a dozen
things besides. In the morning and afternoon she's
a street-crossing attendant at a local school. She's
ideal for the job, for she has a face like a beacon,
and a backside that sticks out like a fender. If
a bus was to go into her, it would get the worst of
the meeting.

About five she came in with a cup of tea.

"I thought it might cheer you up," she said.
"You shouldn't go to cemeteries at your age, you
might be tempted to stay." And she began shivering. "My God," she said, "your room's like a
'fridge. What's the matter? Are you afraid of de-
composing?" She looked around for matches to
light the heater.

"It's no good. It won't light," I said.

She looked at me suspiciously with one eye.
(The other was shut because of a cigarette in the
corner of her mouth.)

"You're not skimping on fuel, are you? I warned
you about that. If you can't afford to buy paraffin
you should go to the National Assistance—"

"I got gallons of paraffin," I said, "enough to
burn. But the heater won't work."

"You're sure?"

17

"Of course I'm sure."

"I don't want anyone in my house perishing of cold. Besides, why are you so afraid of National Assistance? I'm sure I'd screw every penny I could out of those buggers. It's not them who are keeping you, it's you who's keeping them. You've been paying taxes, haven't you, all your bloody life? I'm still paying, through the bloody nose. You earn a bob and you're paid a tanner, and that's as good as a kick up the arse for all it buys. And who gets the money? Not me, mate, nor you."

"Nor me."

"And who do you think gets it?"

"The blacks."

"The who?"

"The blacks."

"That reminds me. Have we had any callers?"

"Callers?"

"Did anyone call about the room upstairs. A chap phoned last night and he said he was coming round to see it today."

"No one came round, not while I was here."

The gentleman called later in the evening. I heard him on the stairs with Mrs. McConnachie. He sounds foreign. I hope he's not black.

It was dark when I woke, very cold and very quiet.
I turned on the wireless: nothing except noises.
It couldn't be half past six yet. My windows were
misted up and I could see a blur of street lights.

It's the thirteenth. Old Stephen never used to
stir out of bed on the thirteenth in case something
should happen to him. In the end something did
happen to him, on the thirteenth. The roof fell
in and buried him in his bed. If whoever it is is
out to get you, he'll find you wherever you are.

I shivered and got back under my blankets. I
could hear a lorry a little away, and then a gate
clanging and rapid footsteps down a stone drive.
That was Jack, a young man in a hurry a few doors
away. And yes, there it was, the sound of him trying to start his motorbike. He wasn't having much
luck. The more he tried the less noise he got out
of it and the more noisy he became. I could tell
how cold it was by the trouble Jack had with his
bike. It must be freezing this morning.

19

I tried to think what day it was. It couldn't be Sunday, because of Jack. It must be Tuesday. They found old Harry on Sunday and buried him the next day, that was yesterday. Must be Tuesday. No, they buried him on Tuesday because there was some sort of to-do with the police and they waited for his sister to come over from Ireland. Yes, it's Wednesday, a busy day for me, specially this week because I hadn't done any shopping yesterday and I had my heater to fix. And there was Choral Evensong at three on the wireless. Me and George weren't great church-goers, but we liked hymns, specially at teatime, and we had Choral Evensong every Wednesday. But was it Wednesday? Didn't they find old Harry on Saturday and bury him on Monday?

George is lucky that way. He can wake up in the morning and without seeing anything or listening to anything he can say to himself, "This is Tuesday," and Tuesday it is. I suppose it's a gift.

I tried the wireless again and twirled it here and there: still only noises.

My sewage wanted cleaning, but the air about me was so cold that the tip of my nose was numb: I didn't know it was there. I've often thought of keeping a chamber pot in the winter, but George had strong feelings on that. "Once you start using a chamber," he said, "you're finished. That's when you want to give up."

"What about the hospitals?" I asked.

"Hospitals is different."

"But you can be taken by surprise even at home," I said.

"Using a chamber for an emergency is one thing, but using it as a convenience is another. No self-respecting man who is master of his own bladder would use a chamber."

When it comes to bladders George knows what he's talking about, for his bladder is what he calls his "Achilles' heel." He's a sturdy little fellow but for that, same as I'm a sturdy big fellow, but for my leg. I also have small troubles here and there, including my bladder and bowels, and aches all over the place, and bronchitis in the winter, but my regular trouble is my leg. I get treatment in hospital every Thursday, same as George has his bladder seen to every Friday. We go down together. He keeps me company for my leg and I keep him company for his bladder. There's three days of the week I can always tell: Leg Thursday, bladder Friday, and Sunday. I have trouble with all the rest.

A noise downstairs! It was Mrs. McConnachie. The whole house shook when she stirred to get out of bed. I could hear her feet on the floorboards now and the lock going "click" on the lavatory door. I wonder why she always locked it. I mean she had it all to herself. I waited for her to flush her toilet. Ah, there it was. It must be half past six. I turned on the wireless: it was. If

my watch stopped, as it did about every half-hour,
I could always tell the time from her movements.
With her about a watch was an extravagance.

There were more footsteps out now, and the
sound of buses and trains. It was still dark, but the
day had begun.

I don't know if I would be able to tell day from
night if it wasn't for the wireless. I remember
George's brother (he's dead now, who isn't?) telling me that when they stopped broadcasting after
the King died he didn't know where he was in the
world, and he remained in bed till they started
again. I wonder what people did before the wireless
was invented. They died younger, I suppose.

My bladder was now pressing so hard that if I
didn't get out of bed soon something would burst.
I braced myself, counted three, threw my blankets
off, swung my legs over the side, and remained
there paralyzed by a jolting pain in my side. I forgot my bladder, my aches, my leg, and began wondering what this could be. My appendix? I had
had it out years ago. Perhaps it grew again? My
liver? Not so far down surely, and not on the side,
and it couldn't be my lungs either. I used to have
a map at the back of a patent-medicine bottle,
like a road map, which told you where everything
was, but I had forgotten it all. The trouble with
me is that I've no sense of direction. Now George
not only knows where everything is, but where by
rights everything should be. He doesn't believe

in God for he believes that if there was a God he would have found a better way of distributing people's organs.

"Now take the sexual organ," he said.

"Take what?" I said.

"The sexual organ—psychologically speaking the most important organ in the body. Can you think of a sillier place to have it?"

"You have to have it somewhere," I said.

"But why there?"

"The body is a botched job," he said, "if you knew something about physiology and anatomy you'd know it was. If there is a God he must have an odd sense of humor, that's all."

Anyway, there I was, pinned to the bed with the pain in my side and dying to get to the toilet. I didn't want to call Mrs. McConnachie, for my pajamas were torn in a strategic place, so I gradually slid down the side of the bed, and pulled myself along the floor on my bottom, like a dog wiping his backside. The exercise or the icy floor helped, for by the time I got to the toilet I was all right again.

A funny thing about the toilet—or the lavatory, the bathroom, the water-closet, the arsenal (Mrs. M's word), the smallest room, the room of rest, the privy, the chair-room, the last resort, call it what you will—is that it's a sort of sanctuary against pain. No matter how bad I've been I've always felt better after a spell on the seat. It's like

23

aspirins, perhaps not a cure, but good enough to keep down the symptoms. The bad thing about it is that it's habit-forming and the more you use it the more you want to use it, till you keep nipping back to it every opportunity like a drunkard to his bottle. I once had a friend (dead now) who read in it, wrote in it, even used to fall asleep in it (or on it). Once he was taken on an old folks' outing to the sea, but he kept going from public lavatory to public lavatory till he was arrested by the police for suspicious behavior. But that didn't cure him either. By the time he died he had a gas-ring fitted up in his lavatory and was having his meals there, and that's where they found him in the end, dying as he lived. He wanted to be buried sitting upright, but that didn't work out for some reason. I suppose it would have made the coffin expensive.

There's not much chance of me going that way, not in Mrs. M's toilet, for the cistern makes a sobbing noise like some poor old soul crying her heart out, and the geyser rumbles, and the taps drip, and she uses a perfumed block to keep the air clean which smells worse (at least to my way of smelling) than anything in the air itself, so that anyone using her toilet for more than ten minutes, if he doesn't pass out, is bound to go round the bend. Sometimes, late at night, if you listen carefully, you think you can hear voices, as if the souls of all the unhappy people who ever lived in the building had been imprisoned in the lavatory. Sometimes

24

there's a gurgle of laughter, like water running down a plughole, but usually there's just this sobbing noise.

I felt much better now and thought the pain must have come from my bladder—perhaps I had caught it from George. Probably not. It was the sort of trouble which came back to me every February, about the time the pipes burst. It had something to do with the frost. Mrs. McConnachie kept complaining about her outdoor plumbing, but it's nothing to the trouble I have with my indoor plumbing—but that's only recent. George has had his for years. He had something fixed about ten years ago, but he doesn't like talking about it, even though I'm his best friend. It's one of those operations which men have in their sixties, the same as that other one which women have in their fifties, or at least so I thought, but one day I asked him straight. "George," I said, "did they remove your balls?" and he had such a fit of laughter that he had to go back to hospital to have his stitches replaced. I can't remember seeing him laugh since.

It was broad daylight now and the traffic outside was roaring like a waterfall.

It was less cold but still icy. I made myself a mug of tea with bread and cheese and had it sitting up in bed reading the Daily Worker, which Mrs. M always passed on to me after she'd read it. When I finished, I dressed and went down to see if there was any post.

There was nothing, not even soap-coupons, not

25

even subscription forms for the Reader's Digest.
I used to get letters from them every week or so
for about six months, and I even wrote to them
once, but I don't hear from them any more. I don't
get the soap-coupons so often either. I would get
one or two a week, but now women come round
with great bags of them at any time of the day,
and that's not the same as getting them through
the post. I don't even get bills. I did the football
coupons for twelve years, but I can't afford them
any more, so that the last time I had any post
was Christmas, and the time before that it was a
census-form or something like that. Sometimes
when I get desperate for post, as I sometimes do,
I write a letter to the Sunday Express saying that
the country is going to the dogs, and I get a flood
of letters back, half of them telling hard-luck
stories and asking for money, and the other half
enclosing copies of the gospel and telling me to
repent.

By the time I got upstairs it was time for Housewives' Choice, a horrible program, all moans and
groans and yeah-yeah-yeahs, but better than Music
and Movement for Juniors which is what they have
on the Home Service.

There was the time when you could hear a decent bit of music on Housewives' Choice, Ava
Maria and Dorothy Squires and things like that
and perhaps a bit of Strauss, but now it's all these
moans and groans. But you can never tell. Only the

other day they had Gallicurchi doing "Lo! Hear the Gentle Lark." George says she's been dead for years, but she still does it as if she was alive. It used to be Elsie's favorite, it and "O for the Wings of a Dove," sung by Master Ernest Lush. You don't hear "O for the Wings of a Dove" on the wireless any more, not even on Family Favorites. She used to love it.

> O for the wings, for the wings of a dove
> Far away, far away wou-oold I ro-ove!

She used to sing it herself sometimes, poor dear, especially when she was ill. She sang a lot then to keep herself cheerful.

"Cyril," she once said, "you know when we die we just can't vanish from the face of the earth, just like that, things don't. We must turn into something. I would like to turn into some sort of a bird."

"What sort?" I asked.

"A dove I think."

"You're a bit big for that, dear," I said, "it would have to be something more like an ostrich." And she laughed till all her gums showed. She was a good soul, and pretty, before she lost all her teeth. Her brothers and sisters had the same trouble and so did her mum and dad. There was never a tooth in the whole family. And she never took to dentures. She said they were dishonest and

27

besides she could never get them to fit. They kept slipping into her soup. That was all years before National Health was even thought of. She was the first woman in our district with false teeth, but she had to give them up after a bit. Funny how quickly you can learn to manage without. George says that the reason people are as big as they are is because they've got all sorts of things which they don't really need, "though they come in useful as spares," he added.

"Cyril! Cyril!"

It was George's voice. He was there by the door shouting through cupped hands.

"Are you deaf?" he shouted. "I've been pressing the door bell for the last ten minutes. It's after ten."

I had been so engrossed with one thing and another that I hadn't even noticed that Housewives' Choice was over, and that Sandy Macpherson was at the organ of some place or another. Funny how he always sounds as if he's in The Chapel in the Valley even when he's in the Granada, tooting.

George calls for me every day on the way to the library, and if he doesn't turn up I know its either Sunday, a bank holiday, his bladder, or he's had a crisis with his Ficus elastica.

Now Ficus elastica is not a subject I bring up often, specially in mixed company, as I am liable to mispronounce it, but it's George's friend and companion, the staff of his old age. I know many people who have gone right through life without ever having come face to face with a Ficus elastica or ever having heard of it, and they didn't seem the worse off for it. And it may be that if I hadn't known George I might never have heard of the Ficus elastica myself.

The Ficus elastica is a house plant, a "rubber plant" some people call it, but you would never hear George call it that. It would be like calling Her Majesty Liz, and Ficus elastica it's been for as long as I've known him.

He used to keep animals, the usual lot, cats, dogs, budgerigars, sometimes one at a time, sometimes all together, but they were all carried off by one plague or another—mostly old age—and about six years ago George turned to house plants. First it was the Nicodemia diversifolia; it lasted a week. Then it was the Phyllitis scolopendrium; it lasted a day. Then there was the Beloperone guttatta. Now that was a more lasting affair. I hardly saw anything of him while that lasted. He was always busy watering it, or dusting, or warming it, or cooling it, and when I did see him, he would talk about nothing else. He was very happy with his little Bella as we came to call it, and the word even got round that Bella was a woman he was living with. And he could have been. He would take it to bed with him on cold nights, or rather he had a little fixture at the bottom of the bed so that he could keep it warm by keeping his toes on it. Anyway,

to cut a long story short, one winter it perished.
George nearly perished with it, and to cheer him
up old Harry and I bought him a Ficus elastica.

It wasn't easy to console him, and he didn't
want it at first.

"No," he said, "Bella was the first plant I've
had any joy with and she'll be the last. I don't want
another." But after a while we talked him into it,
and it's been the Ficus elastica since.

"Feeling better?" asked George.

"Why? Was I feeling bad?"

"You weren't looking too good yesterday."

"Yesterday?"

"At Harry's funeral. In fact, looking at you, I
wasn't sure whether they hadn't buried the wrong
man."

"Was that yesterday?"

"Harry's funeral, when did you think it was?

"Yes, of course it was yesterday, poor soul."

There was a new attendant at the library reading-
room, a dark-skinned fellow with gray, wavy hair.
We had never seen him before.

I was reading the Tattler and Bystander (my
favorite) when George nudged me in the elbow
and whispered, "You get these fellows everywhere,
don't you?"

"Which fellows?"

"These blacks. I mean it's all right having them
on the railways, but it's a bit much putting them
in charge of libraries."

The little fellow looked up, but said nothing.

We had a regular routine, George and me. He started with The Times and I with the Daily Express, and if the weather was too bad for a walk out, we would go through every paper and magazine on the stand, the Angling News, the Baptist Times, the Methodist Recorder, the Jewish Chronicle, the Civil Engineer and Public Works Review, Homes and Gardens, House Beautiful, Vogue, Queen, Britannia and Eve, the Dyer, Textile Printer, Bleacher and Finisher, the Heating and Ventilating Times, the Justice of Peace and Local Government, Dancing Times, the Quarry Managers' Journal, the lot. My memory isn't too good, but George is different. Every passing fact sticks to his memory like a fly to fly-paper and there isn't a thing under the sun that he doesn't know something about. During the war he got as far as the semi-finals in the Home Guard versus the A.R.P. National Quiz.

We had been reading for some hours when George nudged my elbow and, without lifting his head from his paper, whispered, "Look around you."

I looked around me and couldn't see anything in particular.

"You've got no eyes," he said, "look around you again."

I looked around me again.

"Can you still not see anything in particular?"

31

"No."

By now he wasn't whispering but talking, and the attendant came over to us.

"Please," he said.

"Please what?" said George.

"This is a library and not a market. You will have to be silent please."

At this George stretched himself to his full five feet two, took off his spectacles with a flourish, and, looking the man straight in the face, snapped them shut in his case, and strode out. I followed him.

"Now what was that about?" I asked.

George was almost speechless. "The cheek of the man—the cheek of him. I'm not going to be messed around by any black scallywag. That man's father was probably a cannibal, eating missionaries."

"He only asked you to keep quiet."

"He didn't ask me to keep quiet he told me to keep quiet, as if I was a schoolboy."

"Hasn't Mr. Birdie ever told you to keep quiet?"

"Mr. Birdie is different. He's been here for as long as I've been using the library, and he's a gentleman besides. But that scallywag looks as if he's just come out of Africa."

"He looks Indian to me."

"They're all the same; the Indians are more ancient that's all. It means that they've been black longer."

32

"But that's no reason for kicking up a fuss."

"Isn't it? If you knew as much about the subject as I do you'd also kick up a fuss. Did you look around the reading-room when I asked you? You didn't notice anything, did you? You didn't see that nearly every table in the room was taken up by blacks. But you didn't notice, did you? They're hogging the British educational system. Every library you go to is full of them. They're packing the universities. They'll be taking over the country. Take the doctors. Most of the doctors round here are black. Take Dr. Goldberg—"

"He's not black."

"I didn't say he was."

"On the other hand he's not that white."

"I'm not talking about him, it's the fellows who work for him. Remember that time about two months ago when I couldn't get my breathing started? I already thought I was finished but when this great big, black fellow came round I thought my end had come. There I was, lying on my bed, gasping for breath and in he walks. It was a terrible feeling, as if suddenly discovering that God's a black."

When I got back home in the afternoon, Mrs. McConnachie was waiting for me with a cup of tea and a digestive biscuit. A cup of tea she often gives me, but if it's with a biscuit she wants something, and I sat with both hands round the cup waiting for it to come. I knew it wouldn't be a

33

rise in the rent, she'd have given me a slice of cake for that.

"I've got a new tenant," she said out of a corner of her mouth. (She had a cigarette in the other corner.)

"A new tenant?" I said.

"A new tenant, a fine sort of fellow, very educated. He's come with a crate of books so big that it took two men to heave it up the stairs. Very educated, refined type of young man, very."

"He's educated then?"

"Very. It took two men to heave his books up the stairs."

"Fond of reading?"

"He hardly does anything else."

"I like a bit of reading myself."

"I know you do. It'll be like having a public library right on top of you. He's a student."

"A student?"

"Yes, he's studying to study medicine."

"Studying to study medicine, is he?"

"Yes, he's not in University yet, but he's studying to get in."

"Young, is he?"

"Young? Well not by British standards. He might be by foreign standards, though. They count differently there, don't they?"

"Is he foreign then?"

"Yes, I suppose you could call him that."

"Polish?"

34

"Polish?"

"Is he Polish?"

"Why should he be Polish?"

"Because a lot of the foreigners round here are."

"No, he's not Polish."

"Where's he from then?"

"Who?"

"This medical fellow?"

"Medical fellow? Now where's he from again, he didn't tell me. I'll ask him when he comes in later this evening. Very nice fellow, very friendly. I can see you two getting on very well. He's fond of books same as you are. Came with a great crate of them. It took two men to heave them up the stairs. It'll be like having a library on top of you. Makes me wish I had a bit more time to read. But you hardly get the chance to nowadays rushing around from one job to the other. I don't know why I do it. I think it's a habit you get into you know. Once you start rushing around fast enough you just go on and on. You can't stop yourself. Now I once had a sister—"

"Is he black?" I asked.

"Is he?"

"Black."

"Black? Well, now you come to mention it, he's a bit tanned. Comes from a hot climate. You'd be black if your people had lived in India for the past I don't know how long. Being black or white or yellow is just a matter of climate."

35

"And is he going to use my lavatory?"

"Blacks are human same as anybody else you know. They've got bowels and bladders same as you and me. What did Shakespeare say? If we're pricked don't we bleed? And if we drink don't we piss? It's just—What's the matter, Cyril, don't you want your tea?"

I walked straight over to George and found him cross-legged on his bed, like a wise man of the East, with his glasses on the tip of his nose, darning a sock.

"Anything up?" he said, still darning.

"Everything's up," I said. "Mrs. McConnachie's taken a new tenant."

"Why shouldn't she?"

"Wait, I haven't finished. He's a black."

"He's not."

"As black as your galoshes."

With that he put down his sock, took off his glasses, put on his cap, his shoes, galoshes and greatcoat, and we went out in such a hurry that we skidded almost all the way and we arrived breathless and snow-covered.

Mrs. M listened to him in silence, a cigarette smoldering in the corner of her mouth, an eye shut against the smoke.

"Have you finished?" she asked when he had finished.

"I've finished."

"Aren't black people same as you and me?" she began. "Don't they need a roof over their heads same as you and me, and a bed to sleep in? And don't they pay rent the same as you and me, only more regular than some of us. The last fellow who had that room left owing me a month's rent, and that was after raiding the meter!"

"He was foreign," I said.

"He was white. They don't come any whiter than he did, white face, white hair, white everything. I had to wear sun-glasses talking to him."

"Some foreign whites are every bit as bad as blacks," said George. "But two blacks don't make a white. And besides," he added, "what about their women?"

"Their women?"

"Blacks have women."

"And whites don't?"

"Not the same way as blacks."

"In which way do you mean?"

"In which way do I mean?"

"In which way do you mean?"

"I'd rather not say."

"Then stop wasting my time. I'd take blacks in on the principle of the thing, even if I didn't need the money."

"On the principle of the thing? What principle?"

"On the principle that it's my own bloody house and I can do what I bloody well like with it, and if I want to I'll keep blacks, pinks, yellows, blue Persians, White Russians, Catholic Irish, Jews, Armenians, Italians, old lags, young lags, unfrocked priests, juvenile delinquents, unmarried mothers, unmarried fathers, nae'dowells, beatnicks, shitnicks, layabouts, gadabouts, commercial travelers, train robbers, cattle rustlers, horse thieves, runaways, stowaways, shoplifters, undischarged bankrupts, cut-throats, drunks, wife-beaters—"

We left before she had finished and for all we know she may have carried on like that for the rest of the day, for once Mrs. M gets started she finds it difficult to stop.

"I don't think I'll get very far with her," said George. "Women don't listen to reason. It's up to you now. You'll have to make up your mind whether to find new lodgings, or share your old ones with a black. And remember it's not only a matter of sharing the same building. You'll be using the same bathroom, the same bath, and the same lavatory seat."

I thought about it for a long time, so long that it gave me a headache, but I finally decided that I had been living with Mrs. M too long to change.

"All right," said George, "it's your funeral, but there's one thing you can do to help yourself. Buy yourself a very strong bottle of disinfectant and go over the lavatory seat before you use it."

I woke in the night shivering. It was quiet as if
the whole world was caught in ice. I curled up
my legs till they were under my chin but I still
shivered. I couldn't remember so cold a night. I
lit my lamp and got out of bed. The floor was like
ice and the air was so cold it cut. The windows
were patterned with frost and my breath came in
spurts of steam. I took my A.R.P. greatcoat and
put it on the bed, but it didn't help much. I then
took my towel, my raincoat, my suit, almost everything I could lay my hands on except the gas-stove
and sink, and piled them on the bed. That helped
a bit, but just as I was beginning to be comfortable
my bladder began pressing, and I put on my greatcoat, galoshes, and took my bottle of Jeyes in hand
and shuffled down to the toilet. It was locked. It
couldn't be, I thought, not at this hour of the
morning, but then I heard a noise inside, the sort
of noise which can only come from a toilet.

39

George had warned me about blacks not keeping normal hours, but I didn't think they would be that abnormal. I stood there freezing one moment, bursting the next, hopping from leg to leg. He seemed to be in there for the duration, so I rattled the door-handle.

"Other people also want a chance, you know," I said.

"Another minute please," he said. "I have a crisis."

"I'm bursting out here."

"I'm bursting in here."

"These places are not meant to be lived in, you know."

There was silence for a bit, then I heard the paper roller going. He must have used up most of the roll. A good job I had the Daily Worker in my pocket.

He came out a few seconds later perspiring, holding up his trousers with one hand, and a book in the other. He was a small wispy fellow, very black, with straight hair and eyes so deep in his head that I could hardly see them.

"I'm sorry," he said.

I couldn't wait for his apologies but pushed past him and locked the door.

I complained to Mrs. M later in the day.

"I know," she said. "I heard him and I heard you. You shouldn't drink last thing at night. And besides, why don't you use a piss-pot? I don't mind telling you I do, specially in this cold weather."

George came round for tea.

"It's freezing here," he complained.

"I know. A man was supposed to come and fix the heater, but he didn't."

That started him off.

"They've no pride in their work, that's what's wrong with British working men. They've no pride in themselves; they've no self-respect. When I was a lad I earned tenpence a day, and I went to it in the early hours of the morning and kept to it till late at night. This country hasn't got any working men—just layabouts playing at work." And so he went on and on. But he quietened down as it got dark and we sat by the window watching the children on the way home from school shouting, skipping, slithering, pushing, fighting.

"There's the future of Britain," said George. "Makes me shiver to look at them."

The sky was a dark red, as if angry with cold. The street lights came on. We were sitting now in almost complete darkness.

"I'd better turn on the lights," I said.

"No don't," said George, "keep them off. Let's stay as we are."

There were no children in the street now, but a thick jam of buses and scooters and cars moving slowly, trembling, steaming.

"I remember when I saw my first car," he said. "I was twelve then and I thought it was a monster. I ran shouting all the way home and I was afraid to come out in the street for the rest of the day."

41

"I miss the horses," I said.

"Lovely beasts."

"Lovely smell."

"And sound. We lived near a cavalry barracks and they came past our windows in the early hours. Lovely sound, hooves on cobbles."

"Even their droppings had a lovely smell."

"Lovely shape too, like those fancy loaves the Jews have."

"It was never as cold then as it is now, was it?"

"Never. It's all these rockets and things and radio waves. They're cutting the air up into ribbons with millions and millions of radio waves, people sending messages to Australia, and Africa and America and all over the place, it all cuts up the air into smithereens—bound to have an effect on the weather."

"It was never so cold then."

"Never. And do you remember the summers?"

"Blazing hot. Started in May and lasted till October."

"Do you remember that summer when the old king took ill?"

"Yes, I remember. Went to Bognor, didn't he?"

"No, the other one."

"Edward?"

"That's the one, Edward."

"He was a nasty lot though, messing about with actresses and other men's wives. Good for nothing. The country's never been what it was since he was on the throne. He was the worst king Britain's had since Nero."

"Since Nero?"

"Not since Nero."

"Was he British then?"

"No, he was Italian. That was all the trouble you see. The British royal family wasn't really British. Well, it is now because they've been living here all this time, but he was still really foreign, and a low-lifer. Sort of man who shouldn't have been allowed in a respectable man's house."

"Nero you mean?"

"No, Edward."

"I see."

And we remained there quietly until he went home.

*Thick snow. On the window sill. On the bit of
garden in front, on the privet hedge. On the trees,
their topsides white, their undersides black. The
pavement thick with snow, and the cars by the
curb buried in it. The glare was so bright it glowed
through my curtains and onto the ceiling, and
when I drew the curtains I knew I was a prisoner
for the day. Still it's Sunday so it doesn't matter.*

Sunday is my enemy, Sundays and bank-holidays.

"They arrange it so as to drive you into church,"
said George.

The trouble with George is that he's not only
anti-Church, he's anti-drink, in fact he's anti almost anything I can think of. Not that I'm a drinking man myself, but I do like to go into a pub now
and again and spend an hour and a half over a
glass of something or other. But never on Sundays.
On Sundays the pubs are full of jostling, sweating,
red-faced men and fat, noisy women, and I hate
going in, specially by myself. I used to catch up on

44

all the Daily Workers Mrs. M leaves me on Sundays, but now I have trouble with my eyes if I read too long. It's my left eye mainly and I used to try reading with one eye shut, like Mrs. M does when she's having a fag, so now I go visiting on Sundays, to George, to Mrs. M, to old Harry when he was alive, and I do my darning and cleaning up my bits of things.

But in really bad weather I'm stuck, and all because of my leg. The pains I can get used to, unless they get really fierce, but there are times when I want to go one way and the leg keeps turning another, which is a nuisance. It's got a will of its own, and it can turn nasty any time, but especially in bad weather.

"Don't take chances," said Mrs. M. "Stay indoors, and if it's some woman you want to sneak out to, she'd better come and see you. We're all broad-minded in this house."

The wireless isn't very good on Sunday, that's the trouble. It's all women's stuff and hymns. I don't mind Choral Evensong hymns at teatime on Wednesday, but somehow hymns on Sunday is not the same, and I don't like sermons, or "lift up your arse stuff," as Mrs. M calls it. There's The Archers of course, but I hear them every night so there's no point in listening to them again on Sunday morning. And I haven't got a good ear for music. George has, though, that's why he's in most of Sundays. Often as not when I visit him on Sundays he's listening to Bach or something like that and

45

I can't breathe or open my mouth until he's finished.

In fine weather there's the park and I'm there every day, even though it's up a steep hill, but the weather's been bad and I've almost forgotten what the park looks like.

I sometimes do a bit of fancy cooking on Sundays, for I have more time then, perhaps an omelette with a piece of tomato inside, and some rice pudding with jam in it, and maybe a cup of tea and a current bun. I'm not afraid of spoiling myself. Old Dick (he's dead now) inherited quite a bit of money from an aunt who was even older than himself, but he was afraid to spend it. "I'm saving it for a rainy day," he kept saying, "saving it for a rainy day," as if he was always living in bright sunshine. In the end he was knocked down by a bus and it all went to his wife he hadn't seen for twenty-two years. No, I'm not afraid of spending money, I only wish I had it to spend.

I got down to my cooking almost as soon as I got up, not because I had a raging appetite, but because it was the only way I had of keeping warm. The man who was to fix the heater didn't come on Thursday, he didn't come on Friday. On Saturday George helped me to bring it to the shop, but when the man looked at it he said it wasn't worth fixing. So now I've no heater at all: I can't afford a new one, so what I do when I'm at home is either to stay in bed with all my clothes on (except my boots), or I sit and boil myself something on the gas-ring. George says I should ask Mrs. M to fix me up with a heater but if I do she'll start her whole sing-song about the National Assistance and the workhouse and whatnot, and in any case, she happens to be away. I slept in yesterday because I didn't hear her pull the chain.

I made myself a fancy lunch and by the time it was cooked all the windows got steamed up and it got so warm that I was able to take my coat off.

I ate very slowly, listening to Two Way Family Favourites, the news, and Country Questions. And then I cleared up listening to The George Mitchell Singers.

I used to do a bit of singing myself when I was younger, mainly Irish songs, though I'm not Irish myself, at least I don't think I am. My mother was Welsh from a place I can't pronounce and nobody can spell. I probably inherited my voice from her, for she came from good singing stock. My father never said anything much about himself while he was alive and mother never said much about him after he was dead. He could have been Irish, but my Irish songs came from Elsie. Not that she was Irish herself, but she liked Irish songs and she would ask me to sing them.

> Oh, I will take you home, Kathleen,
> To where the roses bloom again,
> To places you have never seen,
> Where you will be my blushing bride.

47

About three the sun came out, a very pale sun and without a bit of warmth, at least none that I could feel. There were children and dogs outside.

I must have fallen asleep, for when I woke it was dark and I was shivering. The street lights were on, but it was quiet and very, very cold. The snow was blue in the lamplight and there were a few cars passing with chains on their tires. I lit both gas-rings and put a kettle on the one and soup on the other. Although I had my greatcoat on and my quilt over my greatcoat and I was standing right over the gas-rings, I was still shivering and I almost felt like putting the flaming jets up my jumper. I couldn't remember it being so cold. My breath came shooting out in spurts of steam as if I was a dragon, and if I hadn't been able to see my nose I wouldn't have known it was there. I made myself a mug of tea and kept my two hands tight about it, sipping slowly.

I was beginning to thaw out when the door bell rang. "George," I thought, but then remembered it couldn't be. He didn't go out in heavy snow, and certainly not after dark, and in any case Down Your Way was now on the wireless and he never missed that.

The bell rang again.

Why did the bloody black not answer? What does he think, I'm his bloody servant?

The bell continued ringing: a horrible, sharp, high-pitched sound. I couldn't stand it.

48

I threw my door open and went upstairs to give the fellow a piece of my mind, but his room was in darkness.

I went slowly downstairs and opened the door. It was a tall, lean man in a trilby hat and shabby overcoat.

He looked at me for some time without a word, then he said, "Where's the old girl?"

"The old girl?"

"Mrs. McConnachie."

"I don't know. She's been away for the past few days."

"Away? Are you sure she's away?"

"Well she's not here."

He pushed past me, went into the hall and tried the kitchen door. It was locked.

"You don't know where she's gone to?"

"No. She comes and goes."

He stood thinking in the pathway for a bit, looked up at me for a moment as if to say something, and was off.

"Shall I say who called?" I shouted after him, but he didn't answer.

She had odd friends, Mrs. M. Of course, he could have been a relative and people can't help relatives. Elsie had an aunt who thought she was a hen and tried to hatch out eggs by sitting on them, and my mother had a cousin, a great, big red-faced man with a shaggy beard who had a voice like a small girl, almost as if he had swallowed one,

49

and who got drowned while crossing on the Wool-
wich ferry. On the other hand old Stephen (he's
dead now) had a sister (she's dead now) who had
a voice like a man, only she had a moustache as
well, so I suppose she was entitled to it.

Mrs. M never said much about herself, but she
was a Mrs. so she probably was a widow, in which
case that fellow could have been her son, though
he looked a bit old for that, and he looked a bit
young to be her husband—and what was she doing
with a husband if she was widowed.

I stopped a long time on the stairs, because for
no reason that I could think of I didn't want to go
back to my room. Usually I was very happy in it.
I could get pleasure sitting up in bed and just looking at it, but now I remained on the stairs in the
dark. It was rather comforting, the dark, though it
was very cold.

It was like this when we first got married, not
the dark or the cold, but we got our house before
we got furniture, and we used to sit like this, with
plates in our laps eating on the stairs. It was a
lovely little house, very narrow. You couldn't move
anywhere without going up some stairs. "It'll help
to keep my weight down," said Elsie. It would have
taken more than stairs to keep her weight down,
poor dear, and she wore a groove in the wall, moving up and down. There was a lot of her, but she
was gold, every bit of her. She had a pretty face, a
bit small compared to the rest of her, and it grew
smaller after she had lost her teeth, but it was pleas-

ant to look at and very kind. But kind people don't last.

She was a bit of a load for that poor heart of hers, and one day just before Christmas we were in town shopping when she suddenly dropped everything she was carrying, and said, "Cyril, I feel odd." They brought her a chair and she sat down, and I got her a glass of water, and as she was drinking it she gulped and her head dropped forward. Somebody called a doctor and by the time he came it was all over.

"It's better that way," my friends kept telling me, "If you've got to go it's better to go quick." And I suppose it is. This is me going slow ever since. It all seems so long ago that I sometimes wonder if it ever happened, if she had ever lived or died, or if we had ever married.

I must have fallen asleep sitting there and then slumped onto the floor, for the next thing I knew I was lying in bed, with the black fellow sitting on the chair beside me.

He had walked in and found me spreadeagled on the floor and got such a fright that he nearly dropped on top of me. He called a doctor, an ambulance, the police, but they found I was only asleep and carried me up to bed.

"Are you all right now?" he said.

"Fine, but it's odd that I should have dropped off like that. It must have been very late. What time is it?"

"Twenty past six."

"In the morning?"

"At night."

"It can't be."

And he showed me his watch.

"It is like an ice-box in here," he said. "I tried to light your heater but I don't know how."

"It's useless, it doesn't work."

"But you cannot live without a heater on a night like this."

"I'm beginning to find that out, but I can't afford a new one and George knows where he can pick up a good second-hand one cheap. He's fetching it tomorrow."

"Wait," he said, and came back a minute later smiling and with a large electric heater in his hand. "Soon you will be all right," he said.

"Soon I'll be ruined," I said, "do you know how much electricity costs?"

"Is it expensive?"

"Expensive? It costs a fortune. It eats money. Last time I had an electric heater I got a pain from bending down putting shillings in the meter, let alone the cost."

"All right," he said, "I'll make you a Christmas present," and before I could stop him he had plonked five shillings into the meter.

"Now where do I plug this in?" he said. "Ah yes, here we are."

I don't know what happened next, but there was a flash, a bang, and we were in complete darkness, and what with him being black and the room being black I could see no sign of him.

"Are you all right?" I said, looking this way and that.

"I'm all right," came a voice from under my bed, "but your wiring isn't."

He fiddled around with the fuse box downstairs without much luck.

"I'm sorry," he said, "there's something wrong."

"You mean to say we're stuck in the dark for the rest of the night?"

"I could try and find some candles," he said.

"A lot of use they'll be. You shouldn't start things you can't finish."

"I'm sorry."

"It's no good being sorry. That won't fix the light."

"I'll find some candles," he said and was off.

I switched the wireless on and sank back in bed. It would soon be time for the Sunday night serial. Then suddenly I realized that the wireless wouldn't be working either. It hadn't occurred to me before. The wireless wouldn't be working. No serial, no news, no Sunday night talk, no late-night dance music, no epilogues, no weather forecasts, just silence. The more I thought of it the darker it grew, and for the first time for as long as I could remember I began weeping, and with a high-pitched sound that I didn't recognize. It didn't seem to be coming from me.

53

I woke up shivering, and with a sharp pain in my side. I wanted to go to the toilet badly but I was too lazy, and it was too cold to get out of bed. I wished I had used Mrs. M's advice and got myself a chamber. George didn't like them, but George didn't have to know. But could I afford one? I was not sure if I could, and it wasn't the sort of thing you could borrow. I did the next best thing, tip-toed over to the sink and used that.

What would George have said to that? Wouldn't be surprised if he did the same thing on the quiet. In fact it wouldn't surprise me if on these cold mornings half the country used the sink if it couldn't get over quickly to the toilets.

It was unhygienic I suppose, but it couldn't be all that bad because the body can't put out any-thing worse than it takes in—only it's a bit pro-cessed. Still, to be on the safe side, I let the taps run for about twenty minutes.

54

My watch was now dead beyond all reviving. There was no sound outside, not even Jack trying to start up his bike. It felt as if the whole world was trapped in ice, and me alone and loose. I shivered at the thought of it. Not a sound. Perhaps I had passed out during the night and I was dead. It could happen. Younger men than me have snuffed it in their sleep, but no, I couldn't have. Dead men don't pass water. Or don't they? Why shouldn't they have to, but if they have to they couldn't be very dead. Besides I suddenly felt very itchy, and I remember somebody saying—I think it was George —I itch therefore I am. I don't mind itching, because if I itch I scratch and I enjoy a good scratch.

I must have been scratching for about ten minutes when I heard the quiet crunch of footsteps in hard snow and a gate closing, and I sat up with my ears ready, waiting for Jack's morning wrestle with his bike, but there was nothing—just the crunch, crunch of feet in snow fading away to silence. He's given up. About time too.

This must be Monday, is it? Yes, it must be, and I sat back in bed thinking over my program. There was the clearing up to do from the weekend, and the shopping, and then the library. There was a serial in The Lady I wanted to finish. George says it isn't a good thing for a fellow of my age to get too tied up in serials.

"Why not," I said, "are you afraid I mightn't make it?"

"No, it's not that," he said. "You see it's all psychological." (With George everything was.) "I know a fellow who began one of these serials and as long as it went on, he went on, but when it finished he found there was nothing he could do with himself, so he died."

Well, if being busy is one way of staying alive, I suppose I could go on for ever, but the thing about the serials is that I could never remember what happened from one week to the next, but still, reading them is like getting to know a new class of people. In fact it gets to the point where the only living people you know are in books, or serials. I like serials more than books because they have more happy endings than books have. Not that I read many books nowadays. Up to a few years ago I used to read two or three books a week, but nowadays every book you pick up seems to be telling the same story only in different words, with everybody aching to get into bed with everybody else. I'm as broad-minded as the next man. I don't mind what people do with themselves, but I don't see why they should write about it, and if they do, I don't see why I should have to read it, especially as I've got trouble with my eyes. And the pictures are getting as bad.

George and me don't go to the pictures much. They're bad for the eyes and the pocket, but we like war films and the other day we went to see a film called Hiroshima something or other, thinking it was about the Japanese war, but there was nothing to it except this pair, in bed together, yattering about nothing in particular. George asked for our money back.

"It's funny how they get sex into everything," said George, "even the bloody atom bomb."

There was quite a bit of traffic in the streets now, and trains in the distance. The Light should be on by now, I thought, and switched on the wireless. And then I remembered, or thought I remembered, for what happened last night, the blown fuse, the darkness, the silence, seemed so far away that I thought it may have been a dream. But the wireless wasn't working. I tried my bedside lamps it was dead, too.

I got out of bed to make myself a cup of tea. No heating, no light, no wireless, but as long as a fellow can still have a cup of tea things aren't that bad. Where there's tea there's hope. So I lit the gas, filled the kettle and was about to put it on the stove when the gas petered out.

I got back into bed and lay down thinking what to do next. This wasn't one of my days. Good weather or bad, bad leg or good, I would have to get out. I would perish if I stayed in all day, and besides there was hardly any food left in the house. I had a potato or two and an onion, but no bread and no pilchards. I would have to get out. Lucky my yearly bout of bronchitis was over and done with. It wasn't easy for me to move, but at least I could breathe.

The daylight was slow in coming. From the

sounds outside, lorries, buses, scooters, trains, I
could tell that the morning was well on the way.
George was due to call at ten but in really bad
weather he was worse off than me, and as he had
heating and a wireless and a fuller larder than me
there was no good reason for him to go out. If anything it seemed to be getting darker now: must be
the fog, thick, black fog. I could almost feel the
taste of it on my tongue and in my throat. I liked
fogs normally, or at least the fog they had in the
old days, the pea-soupers, thick without being bit-
ter, and warm too, like having a blanket round you.
I met Elsie in the fog. I ran into her on a bicycle.
As her father put it, I buckled a wheel, but found a
wife.

She was very apologetic about it, as if it was
her fault, and offered to buy me a new wheel. Not
having much money then (not that I have much
now), I let her. That's how it all began. I used to
give her bicycle lessons, but my cross-bar got into
the way of things, and she didn't do much better
even after she borrowed a lady's bike. The fellow
who designed a bicycle saddle could never have
had a fat girl friend. Still it was fun and we enjoyed the topples more than the rides. There was
the time when her, me and the bike all toppled
over into a canal. It was a blazing summer's day
and we dried out in no time, though she kept
complaining that a batch of tadpoles had got in
where they shouldn't. We got married about then.

But there wasn't much of my family because I
hadn't much of a family (I've none at all now),
but there were all her relatives in dark suits and
dentures, click-clacking away like crickets.

We went to Frinton for our honeymoon. We
had a room right on the front, with the sound of
the sea in our ears all the time—a roll, a clap, and
then, as the waves moved back, a quiet hiss—and
I thought I could hear voices and the door bell,
all coming through hazily as I fell asleep.

There was an odd sharp smell, and, as I opened my eyes, a white ceiling, white walls. My head felt very heavy, and when I tried to lift it, it remained on the pillow, as if it had turned to stone.

"So you're alive then?"

I turned my eyes in the direction of the sound. It was George.

"I came just in time, didn't I? A few minutes later and you would have been out for good. Hullo, are you listening? Can you hear me?

"Just about," I said, and tried to raise myself again. "Where am I?"

"The Garden of Eden," said George. "You're in hospital. You're lucky not to be in the morgue. I dropped by yesterday morning to bring you the heater I promised. I knocked, I yelled, I shouted, but there was no reply, and I was afraid something had happened to you, and it had all right. I called the police. They forced open the door and found you half out of this world in a gas-filled room.

60

What the hell were you doing with yourself in a gas-filled room? What do you think you are, somebody at Oxford? a film star?

"A gas-filled room? There was no gas when I tried to light it."

"And I suppose you forgot to turn the tap off. I got a fright when they brought you out. I thought you were gone. There was at least two bob's worth of gas in that room. And you'll be saving yourself a few bob being in hospital. They look after you well here. It's warm. The food's not bad, and you've got the radio here behind you, and as long as you're in good health there's no better place you could be on a day like this. The snow's frozen hard and the fog's as thick as velvet. I just about got here. I'm not sure how I'm going to get back."

"You shouldn't have come," I said.

"Why shouldn't I?"

"You don't want to end up on a stretcher."

"We all end up on a stretcher sooner or later."

As he was speaking Mrs. McConnachie came puffing into the ward with a bunch of grapes in one hand and a bouquet of chrysanthemums in the other.

"So you're alive?" she said.

"Just about," said George.

"The police have ruined my bloody front door," she said. "Next time you want to kill yourself jump in the river. It's cheaper than gas and surer. And what the hell have you done with the electricity? I leave the house for a couple of days and I find

61

everything in darkness and in ruins. Have you been trying to give yourself the electric chair treatment? Old men are worse than children. You can't leave them for five minutes without them getting up to mischief."

It was over a year since I was last in hospital and I found it difficult to get used to the big meals they served—soup, and lots of it, steamed fish, with two vegetables, fruit pie, and custard. Greens cost a fortune at this time of the year, but these people have money to burn. Stacks of lettuce—lettuce in February.

The fellows in the ward seem much the same as last time. Old men look alike, specially when they're sitting up in a hospital bed, head a little to the side, mouth open. The fellow on one side of me is stone deaf. The one on the other side keeps bending over to tell me things, but his words all get jumbled up in his nose and all that comes out is something like a honk.

They've repainted the place. The walls used to be the color of gravy, but now it's all white and light green—color of peppermint, if peppermint has a color. The smell's changed a bit, too. It used to be Mansion's polish, ether and pish. The ether and pish are still there, but they've changed the polish.

The parson's the same, the fellow with the red face and blue ears who buried old Harry, and the sight of him upset me a bit.

"And what are we doing here?" he said.

"I don't know what you're doing here," I was going to say, "but what I'm doing is—" Instead I was my polite self and said, "I've had a bit of an accident."

"An accident? Have we fallen down and broken something? We shall have to be more careful. Mortal man is a frail creature."

And I told him that I had inhaled two bobs' worth of coal gas, which upset him very much.

"Dear, oh dear," he said, "not in despair I hope?"

"Not in what?"

"Not in despair."

"No, in error."

"Ah, that isn't so bad. One should never take a drastic decision in a moment of despair. All of us find ourselves in the shadow of the valley of darkness at some time in life, but there is a light beyond the shadows—if only one is prepared to look for it. I would say your accident was an omen."

"A what?"

"An omen, a sign that you were spared for something great, good or noble. You may not be a young man but I'm sure you've not exhausted your possibilities."

"Exhausted my what?"

"Your possibilities."

And he bobbed off to the next bed.

If it wasn't for the nights I wouldn't mind being in hospital permanent. About eight o'clock the last of the visitors is away and they begin clearing out

63

the flowers and tidying up your bedside tables, and tucking in the blankets and settling us down for the night. For about half an hour all is quiet, then, as soon as the lights are out the fun begins. First a fellow in the bed next to me begins to fart, not one short noise but a long, drawn-out fart as if his soul is trying to get out through his backside, and while he's busy at one end he sniggers at the other; and somebody else starts to groan, and a third fellow to wheeze, and a fourth one to cough so hard that he sounds as if he might turn himself inside out. And all this time the first fellow is farting and sniggering and three or four others have now taken up groaning as if they're singing a part song. Then somebody wants a nurse and he hasn't the strength to call her so he bangs with his glass on the table and the fellow in the bed next to him takes up the shout, until there are nurses running from all directions.

I must have been good and tired, for I fell asleep through all this. When I woke a bit later I forgot where I was and thought I was in hell, for here I was in a long, dark room, with moans and groans coming from all over the place, and dim, hunched figures stumbling in and out. Then, I heard a gurgling noise from the next bed, and again there was a rush of nurses and doctors. They screened off the bed and then began carting out all sorts of machinery. The gurgling stopped. I waited for a long time to see if it would start again, but it didn't.

I was sitting up listening to nothing in particular when a tall thin fellow in a tattered dressing-gown came wandering down the passageway, and stopped by my bed.

"What are you in for?" he said.

"Gas," I said. "And you?"

"Water."

"Are you?" I said. "I've got a bit of trouble with it myself, but I have a friend who—"

"If it's water," he said, "it can't be a bit, and if it's a bit it can't be water. I've been suffering from water for as long as I can remember. When I'm properly filled up I've got enough in me to float a battleship. When somebody tells you he's got a bit of water trouble it means he's only got a bit of water, and bits of water are quite natural. You're entitled to them. More, you need them. There's more water in the body than anything else. It's a good thing, but you can have too much of a good thing, and that's what I've got."

65

"That's not the sort of water I mean," said I. "My friend's got no more water than he needs, but he can't always pass it off when he wants to, and sometimes it gets passed off even when he doesn't want to."

"That isn't water he's suffering from, it's controls."

"I've always called it plumbing."

"Does he spring leaks?"

"No. His trouble is timing."

"Then it's as I said—controls. My dad suffered from his controls, but there's nothing to plumbing nowadays. All he probably needs is a new washer. But water is the worst of the lot. There's no real cure for water, at least not in the way I have it. All you can do is to suffer in silence, and that's what I've been doing—suffering."

"In silence?"

"In silence."

Visiting-time was slow in coming and when it came George didn't turn up and neither did Mrs. M. I kept looking for their faces in the crowd and after a bit every man I saw began to look like George and every woman like Mrs. M.

Mrs. M has some sort of job most evenings and George, I suppose, was kept away by the bad weather. He wasn't looking too well himself yesterday and at his age and in his condition he's got to watch it, though when he was in hospital last year I didn't miss a day, hail, rain or snow, even though I was only just out myself. The trouble with

George is that he fusses. He's a bachelor, an old maid, and he's had nothing to do with himself all his life except worry about his health and his plants. His brother was even worse. He used to get all the health magazines going and home doctors and all that, and no sooner did he read about an illness than he had it, everything from housemaid's knee to clergymen's sore throat. He used to worry himself and everybody he knew to death, and that kept him going; he had nothing else to do. In the end he thought he was chasing after a bus, and here it was coming towards him, and that was that.

"I beg your pardon."

A young woman with spectacles was bending over me. She thought I had been speaking to her. I had been speaking to myself without even knowing it. My God I was going gaga. Perhaps I had been talking to myself for months without anyone to hear me. No, it was probably this last night in hospital. It had been enough to drive anyone round the bend.

As I was thinking or talking, I don't know which, a sad-looking man with a white face and bad teeth sat down beside me.

"I don't know you," he said, "and you probably don't know me, but I couldn't help noticing that you didn't have a visitor, so I thought I might sit down here for a bit and try to cheer you up. I belong to an organization known as Help Anonymous."

"Help Anonymous?"

"Yes, it's rather an unusual name for a most brilliant idea. Elderly people nowadays are very independent minded, and good for them that they are, but they do need cheering from time to time, and we try to provide the cheer. Now I, for example, make it my pleasant duty to visit hospitals. It comes as second nature to me. I visited my late wife, of blessed memory, every day over a course of seventeen years, and now I come here quite automatically and try to cheer people up as I used to cheer my late wife—and I concentrate on the elderly. I do think they need more cheering than anyone else, don't you? I also try and maintain the contact, so that when an old person is discharged I try and visit him at home—at least that has always been my intention. Unfortunately so few old people are discharged. It isn't that they remain in hospital for ever, but, to use a euphemism, once discharged they are no longer in a condition to appreciate a visit from me or anyone else—if you follow my meaning.

"It is this aspect of our work which is a little depressing, but which makes it all the more necessary. Often I am the last harbinger of cheer, the last mortal face a man sees, before he comes face to face with the Great Visitor himself. If you should survive your unfortunate ordeal, I hope you will not hesitate to look upon me as a counselor and friend, and if this bed should indeed prove to be your last resting place before your eternal one, I would like

68

you to feel assured that you will not be departing
this life without a prayer from my humble lips. Of
course, in a manner of speaking, it is us poor
wretches who remain on this side of the hill who
require every prayer we can muster. The world is a
miserable place, and that is why I feel the old require every consolation for having passed over when
their turn came. My poor wife"—and here he broke
into tears—"was my senior by twenty-two years—
I have always preferred the more mature woman,
you understand—she was a Perkin-Osbalston, and
the Perkin-Osbalstons, as you probably know, have
always tended to expire rather early in life—at least
this is true of the Staffordshire branch of the family: I believe the Warwickshire Perkin-Osbalstons
were prone to longevity—and I braced myself for
the thought that I would be a widower rather early
in life; but I was three decades and six, and she
nearly ninety, before she departed this earth. Although of noble pedigree, her disposition was meek
and I don't think she ever came to the attention of
heaven sufficiently to be struck down. You're probably a meek man yourself are you not?"

"A meek man?"

"You give the appearance of being meek."

"I'm tired."

"I think if you will talk to your contemporaries
you will discover that most men of great age are
meek, hence the saying 'And the meek shall inherit
the earth.' Believe me, my friend, and I speak with

69

experience, the earth is not worth inheriting, and if you should expire in the course of your stay here, as most of your contemporaries are wont, I hope you will count yourself as fortunate." He rose. "It seems that my time is up. I hope I have been able to lend a little brightness to your long night of life." He left me his card. "And if you feel that you may need a kind word, a helpful hand, a cheerful thought, please don't hesitate to contact me. Just dial this number on my card and ask for Help Anonymous. It's me."

I was just fitting on my ear-phones for a bit of music or something, when a small woman came puffing towards me, staggering under a huge blob of a baby, a great big white thing, a good bit bigger than herself.

"I'm sorry I'm late, Dad," she puffed, "but I couldn't find my glasses. I looked for them all over the place and so did Fred, everywhere we've looked but we couldn't find them. I think Winston's swallowed them. He's a very good child, but he swallows everything he lays his hands on, and every time we've got something missing we have to take him for an X-ray. When he was a bit smaller Fred used to shake him upside-down, but he's getting a bit heavy for Fred now. In his condition he's got to watch it, you see. I was going to leave him at home, Winston I mean, but Fred thought he'd cheer you up a bit. Smile at Grandad, Winston, come on, show him your teeth."

70

Winston scowled.

"I don't think he liked the journey. Usually he does nothing else but smile. Come on, Winston, show Grandad your teeth."

Winston didn't.

"Yes, when he was smaller he only ate hairpins, and needles and small things like that. Now it's everything he can lay his hands on, spoons, egg-cups, egg-timers. You know those small bottles of vitamin stuff they have for babies, he's swallowed two of those, bottles and all. He'll be on to furniture next. And he doesn't stop growing. It takes two of us to get him in and out of the cot, and if Fred's feeling tired I have got to call in a neighbor. Fred says we should fix up a block and tackle, but it's a whole business. Come on, Winston, show Grandad your teeth."

But he didn't.

"How are you feeling then, Dad? You look much better, that much I can see. Funny what a week or two in hospital can do for a man. You're not the same person, are you? Yes, you should have had it seen to years ago. Fred says they've got cures for everything, except what he's suffering from. His trouble of course is that they don't know what it is. All they do know is that he's got to watch it, and he does. He knows how to look after himself, Fred. He's not reckless. You wouldn't call him reckless, would you, Dad? I wouldn't. If he knows he's got to watch it, he watches it. He's a good bit better

71

you'll be glad to hear. In fact he wanted to come with me, but you know what buses are like at this time of the night, so I said he'd better not. I mean people'll get up to give me a seat at least if I'm with Winston, but they wouldn't get up for him.

"There's no way of telling that Fred's got to watch it, at least not by looking at him. Yes, I'm glad to see you looking better. You must admit that if it wasn't for Fred you'd still have been moping around with your hand to your side as you'd been doing for months. It was Fred's idea. Have it seen to, he said, for once and for all, or you'll be a misery to yourself and a misery to us for the rest of your life. You're looking much brighter, much. I can't help thinking if mum had gone in when Fred said she should she'd also have been a different person. She might still have been alive now. Well, I'd better be off, Dad. It takes me nearly an hour to get back and Fred likes some hot cocoa before he turns in, he's got to turn in early on account of his condition. Kiss Grandad, Winston, come on, Winston, kiss him. I said kiss him."

And she pushed his great, big, blubbery face into mine, and was off, half carrying, half dragging him.

My room was full of surprises when I got back. There was a great big lump of sultana cake from Mrs. M with a welcome-home card. And the room was warm. There was a new paraffin heater there, or rather an old one which George had got for me, but it was working and the cosy smell of the paraffin was the best welcome I could have had.

I took off my coat, hat and shoes, put on my galoshes, filled the kettle, and was going to light the gas, when I found that there was none. The gas-ring had gone and in its place was a small electric stove. I kept putting matches to it for five minutes before I found out that it was electric. She might have told me, the silly old bitch. It's all right her buying me electric stoves, but it's me who has to pay for the electricity. Besides I'm used to the gas-rings. I can do miracles with them. The meals I've made on my two rings you couldn't get in the best hotels. And I liked the smell of gas, and even if a

73

little of it escaped it wasn't so bad—mixed with floor polish it was very nice on the nose.

I was so upset about the rings that I didn't put the kettle on. I didn't even switch on the wireless, but sat there moping in my chair. It was her gas-ring, but she might have asked me before she threw it out.

As I was sitting there, there was a knock on the door and a black fellow put his head round the corner.

"Welcome home," he said; "are you feeling better?"

I just sat there and looked at him.

"You are looking better," he said; "how are you feeling?"

He was right inside the room now.

"Do I know you?" I said.

"Me?"

"Have we met before?"

"I'm Sayed. You remember? My electric heater? I put it in there. Bang. Darkness. Last week?"

And then I remembered. I quickly went over to the wireless and switched it on. It was working, thank God for that.

"Are you feeling better?" he asked.

"Yes, I'm feeling better, not that I felt so bad in the first place. I don't know why they had to cart me away to hospital. It's no place for a healthy man. They nearly drove me round the bend. Here, do you know anything about the gas-rings?"

74

"Gas-rings?"

"Yes, I had a pair of gas-rings and they're both gone. She's left me some sort of electric stove in their place. They're useless these things. Take hours and cost a fortune."

"No, I don't know anything about them."

"I've a good mind to go out and buy myself another pair. You wouldn't believe it if I told you the sort of things I could make on gas-rings—not that I do now everything's so expensive. But I used to, and I'm used to them. I'm a gas-ring type. These small stoves are women's things, for widows and spinsters and that."

"I'm sorry I don't know anything about them."

"You don't happen to have a pair of rings in your room?"

"No, she took them away. I'm also all electric now."

"I bet she's got gas in her own room. I bet she has. It's good enough for her, but we've got to make do with electricity. It costs a fortune electricity does. I've a good mind to nip out and buy myself a pair of rings. I'm sure I could pick up a second-hand pair for a couple of bob—not that a couple of bob is something to be sneezed at, but they'll be mine then and she won't be able to—"

"But she's had the gas-pipes stopped up—look along there, can you see?"

And so she had.

"That's spite, you know, nothing but spite. She

knows I like gas and that's what she goes and does. I wonder what she would say if I corked up her pipes, and I've a good mind to."

"The gas is dangerous you see—"

"And electricity isn't? I bet there's a dozen fellows electrocuted for everyone that's gassed. I bet—" Then I remembered something.

"What time is it?"

"Ten past three."

"And what day is it?"

"Day?"

"What day is it?"

"Wednesday."

I turned the wireless up and put the kettle on.

"It's Choral Evensong," I said; "never miss it. Would you like to hear it?"

"What is it?"

"Listen and you'll hear."

And he listened for about a minute, then he said, "It is very nice, but I have to go to a lesson. It is very nice indeed." And he almost ran out of the room.

I didn't listen for long myself. First of all the kettle took hours to boil and Evensong without tea isn't Evensong. And then I was worried about George. He hadn't turned up at hospital yesterday, and he wasn't there today. Here it was after three on Wednesday, Choral Evensong time, and he hadn't turned up. It wasn't like George, and the more I thought about it the more I worried. Finally I put on my coat and hat and went out.

He doesn't live far from me, not more than ten minutes walk in good weather and perhaps twenty in bad, but I hadn't gone far before I found myself in a street which I didn't think I had seen before. They had been knocking some old houses down and putting other ones up and I couldn't recognize where I was. I took one turning, and then another and then tried to get back to where I was. But I was lost, not more than ten minutes away from home and I was lost. A policeman saw me turning this way and that.

"I'm a bit lost," I said. "I'm looking for—for," and tried to remember where George lived but couldn't think of it. "It's a street full of large red-brick houses, with a church at one corner and a pub at the other."

"They're all red brick round here," he said, "and they've all got churches at one end and pubs at the other."

"There's a fish and chip shop too, and a green-grocers."

"There's fish and chip shops and greengrocers in every street. Perhaps I'll know the fellow. What's his name? What does he do?"

"He does nothing. His name's George."

"George who?"

"George what?"

"George who?"

"Who? George, George. You know, it's a funny thing. I can't remember him using his second name, and if I ever knew it I don't know it now."

"What does he look like?"

"Small little bent fellow, looks like a bird, very old. Almost gaga."

The policeman scratched his chin for a bit, then said, "I think the best thing for you to do would be to go back home, wouldn't it?"

"Back home?"

"Yes."

And I turned to do just that, and went this way and that, but I wasn't sure which direction home was.

"Have you forgotten where you live now?" he said.

"No, I haven't forgotten that, but if only I knew where I was now I would know how to get back."

"Do you remember the address?"

"The address?"

"Where you live."

"I'm trying to think. I must have it written down somewhere." And I began rummaging through my pockets.

"Have you got your pensions book?"

I had, and he led me all the way back to the house and didn't leave me till I was upstairs in my room. It was nearly dark then. I took off my shoes and coat and got into bed, and lay there doing nothing, not sleeping, not thinking, just lying there. There were tears coming down my face. I was crying though I didn't know what was making me cry.

I must have been lying like that for hours when I heard a voice calling downstairs. It was George.

I rushed downstairs so quickly that I got a pain in my side which paralyzed me for a minute.

"Are you there?" George kept shouting. "Are you all right?"

"I'm fine," I shouted. "Can't you wait a minute?"

I opened the door and found him outlined against the street lamps, shivering, with his collar up and a bunch of flowers in his hand.

"You're home then?"

"Of course I'm home."

"Then why the hell didn't you tell me? I dragged all the bloody way to the hospital for nothing."

The kettle was boiling by then and we sat down and had a cup of tea. We were sipping quietly, or not so quietly, when George suddenly said, "We're over the hump you know."

I looked up from my cup. "Over the hump?"

"We're over the hump. The worst of the weather is over. See that blizzard we had last week? Came straight from Siberia, that's Russia, as I suppose you know. Funny how many nasty things come from Russia if you come to think about it."

"Nasty things?"

"Loads of them. There was that weather to start with, well that's over and done with, thank God. Then there's Communism. That's Russian. Then there was the Tartars, you won't have heard of them—"

"I have heard of them. Who hasn't heard of Tartars? Of course I've heard of them."

"These were Tartars, proper, though—pillaged and raped wherever they went—a nasty lot. Well, they're from Russia. And do you remember the Spanish 'flu?"

"Remember it? It nearly killed me."

"Well, it's Russian."

"The Spanish 'flu Russian?"

"I thought you'd be surprised. It broke out about the same time as the Russian Revolution. Now I know something about the Russian Revolution, because my older brother Sam was sent to put it down. He didn't, of course, but I learned a lot about Russia from him, even a bit of Russian. And it was he who told me about the Spanish 'flu. He's seen it at first hand. It isn't surprising the revolution breaking out in Russia. I mean we wouldn't stand for that sort of thing in this country. I know I wouldn't, would you?"

"Would I what?"

"Would you stand for a revolution?"

"A revolution?"

"You wouldn't stand for it, would you?"

"No, I wouldn't."

"Exactly, but in Russia after what they go through every winter, they'll stand for anything. It's all psychological, you see."

"They have long winters then?"

"They hardly have anything else, and sometimes it spreads, like it did last week. But that's all over, thank God. We're over the hump."

80

"Over the hump?"

"The worse of the winter's over. We might even be able to make the park tomorrow."

"The park?"

"Why not?"

"I've almost forgotten what the park looks like."

"Yes, we should be able to go there tomorrow—after the hospital though—tomorrow's Thursday. Yes, I think we should be able to go there after the hospital. This time last year we had the crocuses out, do you remember?"

"Did we?"

"Yes, this time last year, crocuses sprouting all over the place. We had daffs early in March. We won't get them that early this year though."

"No, not this year."

"Do you remember after Dick's funeral we walked home through the park—so warm I had to take my coat off—and the crocuses were just beginning to push their heads through the ground, and you found it very upsetting?"

"I did?"

"Don't you remember? Dick had asked you to wheel him to the park, and you couldn't because of your leg, and by the time your leg was better, Dick was worse. He never did get round to the park."

"And where were you at the time?"

"Where do you think I was, in hospital. I only got out in time for the funeral."

"And was that a year ago?"

81

"Almost to the day."

"Poor Dick."

"Yes, we should be out in the park tomorrow, and about time too. February's nearly over."

"Is it?"

"Nearly over."

"When does the tea-room open?"

"In the park?"

"Yes."

"Not until Whitsun. You don't mean to say you'd use it? They charge you sixpence a cup—sixpence for one cup."

"No, but about the time the tea-room opens, you get the squirrels running wild round the terrace."

"You get squirrels at all times of the year—except in winter."

"But they don't start running wild till the tea-room opens. They come for the crumbs."

"Squirrels don't eat crumbs."

"These ones do."

"You're thinking of mice."

"In which case they're mice with bushy tails. These ones eat crumbs, they ate them out of my hands."

"In the park?"

"In the park."

"I don't remember seeing squirrels eating crumbs out of your hands in the park. I don't remember seeing them eat anything out of your hands in the park."

82

"You don't remember."

"I don't remember."

"That's because you're going gaga."

"I'm going gaga?"

"You're going gaga."

"Well, I'll tell you something. You don't have to go gaga, you've always been gaga."

"If I have, I haven't been half as gaga as you've been. And you're more than gaga, you smell. You stink. You leave a trail of water everywhere you go. Every time you're here Mrs. McConnachie's got to go over the stairs with a mop."

He didn't say anything, but got up white-faced and staggered out of the room. He slipped on the stairs, picked himself up and went out.

He was hardly out when Mrs. M came in.

"Hullo, hullo," she said, "what's been happening? Lovers' tiff, eh? The course of true love never did run smooth."

I knew he'd be in the library and he was, with his cap on the table, his pointed head poking through his white hair, and his feet crossed under the chair.

I went over and looked at the papers first of all on the reading stands, but I didn't do much reading for I kept on wondering how to begin. I wasn't going to apologize because it was him who started the quarrel in the first place. He knew a lot, but it didn't mean to say that he knew everything. If I had squirrels eating crumbs out of my hand, I had squirrels eating crumbs out of my hand. But I had no right saying he stank, especially as he does stink.

I decided the best thing to do was to pretend nothing had happened, so I took Harper's Bazaar out and sat down beside him.

"How is the old Ficus elastica?" I said.

He looked up, squinted at me for a moment, and without speaking took off his glasses, put on his cap, and went out.

84

It was all right with me. I did my Christian bit. I was willing to forgive and forget, and if he wasn't that was his look-out. I remained in the library for a bit, looking through Harper's Bazaar, Vogue, and Queen, treated myself to a meal of fried eggs and baked beans, steamed pudding and custard and tea, at Frank's café just down the road from the library, and went to the pictures. I felt that with all those days in hospital I deserved a treat.

The film was about this French school-teacher who wanted to get rid of his wife, but instead of poisoning her or bashing her on the head like any sensible fellow would have done, he tried to scare her out of her wits. I'm not sure if he did or didn't for I fell asleep after a bit, and when I woke up it was nearly over. I would have slept right on to the very end, but I was wakened by the snoring of the fellow next to me, and when the lights came on who should it be but smelly little George. I don't know if he didn't see me or pretended not to see me, but he put on his cap and went quickly out.

"Well," said Mrs. M when I got back, "have you two made it up yet?"

"He's a difficult little fellow, George," I said. "I think being old and little makes him like that, and he wasn't much better when he was young—not that he ever was. He's been the same size and about the same age for as long as I've known him, and he's always been difficult. I don't think he's on speaking terms with anybody else except me, and he doesn't speak to me now. That's why he reads so much, you see. He can't quarrel with books, though he tries. If you ever watch him you can see him have a quiet grumble to himself at every page. He never married you see, that's his trouble. He's never had to learn. Doesn't even know how to live with himself. It's not as if I weren't ready to make up. I put out the hand of friendship, and he gave it the blind eye."

"He cold-shouldered you."

"Yes, he did."

"You turned the other cheek—"

"I did."

"—and he sent you home with a flea in your ear."

"No, he just pretended I wasn't there."

"That wasn't nice of him."

"But that's him all over."

"I wouldn't worry, you'll forget about him. You want to get yourself a nice girl. The more mature type of male is very much in fashion nowadays, if you haven't heard. Now's your chance. Another year or two and you'll be over-ripe. But see she's the right type of girl, you wouldn't want anyone to marry you for your money."

Funny she should say that about me marrying again. Elsie said I should—before she died that is. "If anything happens to me, Cyril," she said, "I don't want you to stay single," and a week later something did happen. But it takes two to get married. I was willing if I could find somebody who

86

was, but in any case I didn't feel like looking, and
somehow I've been living in a men's world all my
life. My mother and Elsie were the only two women
I had known at all well, and I didn't know them all
that well either. But apart from them the only
women I knew well enough to chat with were the
W.V.S. tea ladies during the war. I was a french-
polisher in a furniture factory till I retired, and there
were no women there. In fact, since Elsie died Mrs.
M was the nearest thing to a woman that I knew.
Not that I missed knowing them. I had twelve years
with Elsie and every year of living is good for at
least two years of memories, and I could manage
with that.

I think the winter's over. I could move round my
room, make my bed, clear up, read the papers, listen
to the wireless, without any heating at all. I did have
to keep my coat on, but wearing coats costs nothing: heating does. There was less snow last year,
but I remember I had to keep my heater going till
Easter. If it was only a bit drier I would have been
able to go to the park.

I waited in till about eleven, to see if George
would call for me on the way to the library, but he
didn't—not that I expected him to—and I went on
myself. There was a small fellow like him bent over
the table, but it wasn't him. This fellow smelt of
bad socks, while George smelt of bad plumbing,
and he was asleep, which is something George never
did—not in the library. I remained there all morning and there was no sign of him. Out of curiosity
I went back in the afternoon, but he still wasn't
there, lots of other old characters, though, tramps

88

and layabouts who looked as if they hadn't washed in weeks. That's why George and me usually did our reading in the mornings. You had a finer type of people then, black mostly, but decently dressed—but I suppose it's difficult to tell with them whether they washed or not.

It had grown a good bit colder by the time I got back home, and though I still had my coat on I had to put on the heater. Still, the day was nearly over, and I had saved myself something.

It seemed odd not having tea with George, not that the tea tasted the worse for it, but it just felt odd. Usually he'd sit with his hands round his cup, looking into space and talking. I didn't always listen, but I liked to have the background of him talking to my tea—except on Wednesday, when we had tea early and listened to Choral Evensong. It was about five now, and with hardly anything worth hearing except Children's Hour. I listened to that, and to the news and to the odd bits and pieces they have after that, and to The Archers and to Radio Newsreel.

That's when I normally have supper. As soon as The Archers is over, I put on the kettle and lay the table, and by the time Radio Newsreel is half-way through, I'm half-way through my supper. But I couldn't be bothered now. I sat in my chair with my cup still in my hand, not even listening. He was probably making himself some fancy dish and listening to the Third Programme. He hardly listened to anything else—he even bought the Radio Times to see what was going on. I wonder what he did with himself before the Third Programme was invented. But he was good at cooking, comes from being a bachelor all these years I suppose. I can do fancy things if I want to, but usually I throw everything I have in the room together, put jam on it, wash it down with a cup of tea, and I'm all right. He steams things and grills them and poaches them, and gives them French names. There was a time when whatever you started to chat about, you'd end up talking about his mayonnaise.

His brother Sam was different: same father, same mother, same trouble with the bladder, but different as chalk from cheese. They didn't speak to each other, of course. I was their go-between. I don't know why they had quarreled, but George being George it couldn't have been difficult.

The wireless was going all the time I was thinking and it gave me a headache, and I moved my chair over to the window. It must have been after eight, for there was little traffic. It had stopped raining, but the roads were still glossy, and the few cars that passed glistened like fish. It was cold, but there was no ice or snow. Tomorrow if it was dry I'd go to the park. I could even go there if it was wet. A bit of rain wouldn't kill me, and if it won't something will and I might as well be killed by rain as anything else. Besides, there's a shelter in the park.

90

George never liked to go near the shelter. "It's full of stinking old men," he used to say. "They're past it, they've nothing to do with themselves but rot, and rot is infectious." Can't say he was far wrong though. We were caught in a downpour one April morning and we took shelter inside. The air was brown with a haze of tobacco, snuff, old socks, and sewage trouble. They had all been yattering together loudly, but as soon as we came in they stopped, and they did nothing but gape at us with screwed-up eyes and open mouths. And the moment we left they started again. It was like some private club. "A week in there," he said, "and you'll be as bad as the worst of them." But sheltering for a morning wouldn't do me any harm, and it's right by the flower beds. The crocuses must be out by now, and perhaps the daffodils too. At all events the winter was over.

As I was undressing for bed, it occurred to me that I hadn't had supper—or had I? I decided to make myself an extra big cup of cocoa to be on the safe side.

That was her favorite drink, cocoa. There was the time she was trying to slim and she gave up almost everything, but not cocoa. "It would make me unhappy," she said. "What would you rather have, a wretched slim wife, or a happy fat one?" What I had then was a wretched fat one, for she didn't take to slimming, poor dear. Size of a person goes with character and she would have looked odd in a slim body, in the same way as George would look odd in a big one. Being small is part of his personality, as being big was part of hers.

I used to drink gallons of cocoa during the war. I was reckoned to be about the best cocoa-maker in the A.R.P., at least down our way, and that was on powdered milk. The secret was in the paste. If your milk and water paste was smooth you had good cocoa. If it wasn't, it came lumpy, and there's nothing worse than lumpy cocoa. We used to have it after the nine o'clock news. What's happened to those fellows, Alvar Liddel, and Bruce Belfrage, Frank Philips, John Snagge? You don't hear them much, or much of them nowadays. I suppose they're all old-age pensioners huddled round their paraffin-stoves like myself. The news isn't what it used to be either. Hardly worth listening to, all walk-outs, sit-down strikes, and stand-up strikes, balance of payments, nuclear disarmament, and rot of that sort. News was news in those days.

Little George would make a nuisance of himself even then. If Alvar Liddel or one of the others would mention a place—Smolensk, Kharkov, whatever it was, wherever it was—up would pipe George from his corner with some bit of inside knowledge, like: "Yes, they'll never take that town. It's got a river half a mile wide, with a swift current. All the bridges are down so they'll never get their armor across." Or, "They'll have to pull back now. They're stretching their lines of communica-

tions beyond their limits." Mind you we listened
to him with respect. There would be the news,
then the commentary on the news, then George
with his commentary on the commentary. About
the time Tobruk fell we all felt that George should
have been made Supreme Commander Middle
East Forces. Harry used to think he was a pocket
genius, and whenever he spoke he used to watch
him with mouth open. Though, mind you, he always did have his mouth open. His ears weren't in
good working order and I think he tried to help
them out with his mouth—but that was after
George had told him that the ears, nose, and throat
were all connected.

There were sofas there, not sofas really, but up-
holstered seats from old tram-cars. It got warm
with the coke fire and the smell was sharp and
tickled the nostrils. We would all drop off after
a while. Sleep was never as sweet as it was then.

I don't sleep badly now, but it's all a little taste-
less. I seem to peter out into darkness. Still, that's
better than taking pills. Poor Philip (he's dead
now), he'd have pills for everything: pills for going to sleep and pills for staying awake, pills for
passing water and pills for stopping water, pills for
headaches, heartburn, neuralgia, backache. There
wasn't an organ in his body for which he didn't
have some pills. He was a walking chemist's shop;
he'd rattle with them, half of them to start things
and the other half to stop them. I wonder he never

93

got them mixed up. I shouldn't suppose it mattered if he did. They all canceled each other out and in the end he was canceled out. Poor Philip. (He's dead now.)

I'm not perfect myself. I have a few bottles about the place for this and that, and I need servicing every now and again, but I've got everything I was born with, except my teeth. I find getting around a bit difficult, but that's because I'm a bit big, or rather lopsided, but I always was for as long as I've known myself. No, taking one thing with another I'm in good working order—touch wood.

The traffic was quiet now. Must have been about nine. It's the quietest hour of the day. You've got cars roaring into town till about eight, and they start roaring back from town at about ten or eleven, but about nine hardly anyone moves. It was very quiet, so quiet that I didn't want the wireless on. I opened the window and the curtain billowed in the breeze. The streets were still wet, still glistening. The curtains filled up and emptied, swung inwards and outwards. It seemed much warmer. The winter was over. Tomorrow I would go to the park.

I woke shivering in the early hours of the morning. I had fallen asleep on top of my bed with my clothes on. I changed into my night-clothes and dived into bed. I don't know how long I slept, but when I next opened my eyes the room was flooded in light. It stunned me. I closed my eyes again and blinked them open gradually. I could have done with a pair of sun-glasses. But it wasn't the sun which was flooding the room. It was snow. It lay piled up on the window sill, on the window frame, on the hedge, the trees, everywhere except the road where the traffic had churned it up into a muddy river.

Somebody and his Viennese something or other was playing waltzes on the wireless. I reckoned it was Music While You Work. Half the day was over. From then on I could do nothing right. I never can if I start the day wrong, and I need an early start to the day. By eight o'clock I like to be at my breakfast, washed, cleaned, and shaved,

95

listening to the news. Now I couldn't get the
geyser to light, I cut myself shaving and, worst of
all, when I tried to light the heater—my hand
shook so badly it took me all my time to get the
match to the wick—it flickered and fumed, but it
wouldn't go on. I had used up a box of matches
before I thought of looking if there was any paraffin left. There wasn't, and I had none in the can.

In the old days when I had my gas-rings I could
always get a bit of warmth from them, just sitting
beside them with a kettle on the boil. You couldn't
do that with the electric stove. You'd perish before the kettle ever boiled, and that's apart from
the price. Snow or no snow, there was nothing for
it but to go down to the ironmonger for some paraffin. He wasn't far off, thank God.

I like the ironmongers. It's the one place in town
which always looks like it did and smells like it did:
soap, floor polish and paraffin and ammonia. I used
to go there sometimes just to inhale for old times'
sake. It's called Marks, Mawkins and O'Meara—
like a firm of solicitors. Marks is dead and O'Meara
is dead, but Mawkins is still alive, with his nose
running and his eyes running, and one hand wiping the one or the other. He's got a bad-tempered
fat girl working for him, but Mawkins himself is
a pleasant enough fellow and always good for a
chat. In fact I'm sorry when the paraffin season is
over, there's nothing I really want from him. I've
often thought it would be nice to need a set of

door-handles, or a fireside curb, or one of those little brass tongs, brush and poker sets he has, or a
pair of earthenware Alsatians. But paraffin's the
only thing I need and paraffin's the only thing I
buy. And I think it's the same with everyone else.
He more or less lives on paraffin.

George says he's heard things about Mawkins
and the fat girl, but then George has heard things
about everybody. I suppose he kept her on for
something and it wasn't the help she was in the
shop. Looking at him you'd think he didn't have it
in him, but looking at her you wouldn't think he'd
want it even if he had. Still, who am I to judge?
We all do things in private we wouldn't like to be
caught doing in public. We all pee in the sink in
one way or another. Speaking for myself, if I had
to choose between that girl and the sink, I'd choose
the sink any day.

She was alone in the shop when I came in, like
a cottage loaf in a floral overall.

"Paraffin?" she said.

"What was that?"

"I said paraffin."

"Paraffin?"

"Paraffin."

"Yes, please. You'd think by this time of the
year I'd manage to do without, or at least with less
of it. But look at it now, eh? Look at it. Middle
of spring and we're back to mid-winter. I remember—"

97

"How much do you want?"

"Pardon?"

"How much do you want?"

"How much do I want?"

"How much paraffin do you want?"

"Paraffin? Yes, well, I'd better have about half."

"Half a gallon?"

"Half a tin. How much does half a tin hold?"

"Half a gallon."

"That's what I said, didn't I?" and she grabbed the tin from my hand and went over to the oil drum.

"Arthur not in?" I said (Arthur's Mawkins's first name).

"He's out," she said.

"Yes, I don't blame him from not coming in on a day like this. I wouldn't either if I didn't have to. Do you notice how the winters are getting longer and colder? It's from all that messing about in the outer atmosphere—or is it the upper atmosphere? It's one of the two I'm sure. You can't mess about with the upper atmosphere and expect nothing to happen. That's where the weather is, in the upper atmosphere. Don't ask me what it's doing there, but that's where it is, and if you keep sending up those what do you call 'em you're bound to upset something. And that's what they've been upsetting, the weather. As George put it, it's like having a foreign body inside you. Now supposing you had a foreign body inside you—"

"Anything else?"

"What's that?"

"Do you need anything else?"

"Do I need anything else? Well as a matter of fact I do. A loaf of bread and a tin of pilchards, but you don't sell them here, the more's the pity. I'm fond of pilchards. I've never been able to work out what family—what fish family that is—they belong to. Now they're a bit short for herrings. On the other hand they're a bit too long for sardines, and they're not sprats either. We used to get a lot of them before the war, sprats, but I hardly see them now. Do you remember—"

"That'll be one and tenpence."

"What's that?"

"The paraffin's one and tenpence."

"It's gone up again, has it?"

"It hasn't."

"Well it feels as if it has. Everything keeps going up nowadays, except pensions and spitting in the bus, and who wants to spit in the bus. I haven't been in a bus for years: at least not in a public bus. I remember when—"

"There's nothing else you want then?"

"What's that?"

"There's nothing else you want?"

"I could do with a tin of pilchards—"

"We don't sell pilchards."

"I was just going to say that."

"That'll be one and tenpence then."

99

"One and tenpence?"

"The paraffin's one and tenpence."

"Has it gone up then?"

"No, it has not gone up." And she grabbed the money from my hand, flung it in the till, and almost frog-marched me out of the shop.

It was slippery out, and if I fell once I fell a dozen times, but the worst thing was, when I got back to my room, the stove wouldn't light. I fanned it and shook it and rammed it and banged it and filled it brimful of paraffin. It flickered and fumed, but it wouldn't stay on. I worked on it for more than two hours, and by the time I was finished, I was in a state to pour the paraffin all over the room and set a match to it. The effort kept me warm, but as soon as I stopped the cold hit me. I went down to Mrs. M. I don't know if she would have been any help, but she wasn't in in any case. I went up to the black fellow. He was out.

"Still," I said to myself, "the light is still on and the wireless is working. Things could get worse." And at that moment the lights went off and the wireless stopped.

Snow, getting black and messy, but still thick on
the pavements and high on the hedges. I was going to phone the hospital to tell them I couldn't
come for my leg, but Mrs. M is out so I couldn't
get to her phone, and by the time I got to the outside phone box I decided I might as well skid on
to the hospital. It took me nearly an hour to get
there, and when I got there I found I had come
two days late, or five days early, whichever way
you like.

"Remind me to get you a calendar for Christmas," said the nurse.

As if the cold and snow were not enough it got
foggy early in the afternoon and by the time I was
sitting down to my tea, it was pitch black. My
paraffin-stove still wouldn't light, so I kept the
electric cooker on with kettles simmering on it all
the time, and sat there watching my savings go up
in steam.

101

"Our special account," Elsie had called our savings, "it's all for something special," and this was it, simmering kettles on a foggy afternoon.

I spent a long time over my tea listening to the kettles simmer, when I heard the front door bang shut, a coughing and spluttering, and then footsteps on the stairs.

It was the black fellow. He had kept me awake half with his coughing. I suppose he's never seen snow where he comes from, all heat and sand. Of course it serves him right for coming here in the first place. He's not built for this sort of weather, any more than I am for his. People are like plants, as George always said, you don't try to grow cabbages in a hot-house or peaches in a cabbage patch. I remember old Harry telling me that when they first went out to India the men fell like flies. More of them dropped from the heat than from bullets. Well, if Indians come out here they can't expect to do any better, not even if they're Pakistanis. There he goes again, coughing himself to a frazzle.

Of course they don't have any National Health there as they have here; I suppose that's why they come here. Britain's about the best place to be sick in on earth. And they can't be all that healthy, not when they're that color.

I had just finished clearing up after supper when I remembered that I had over a half a bottle of cough mixture left over from my last cough and I took it upstairs.

He had a dressing-gown over his clothes with a towel round his neck and a towel on his head, looking like a maharajah, and bent over a table full of books.

"I couldn't help hearing you cough," I said, "and I thought you might like a drop of this. It's helped with every cough I've had and as I haven't been coughing lately I have a bit to spare. It's very good. As a matter of fact it was prescribed by a colored gentleman like yourself."

"Thank you very much indeed. But I have a bottle up there: I have three bottles."

"Yes, there's safety in numbers I always say. In the good old days when the National Health began I used to come away with an arm-load of things on my prescription, but they charge you two bob a time now—two bob. You can get a tin of pilchards for that and have enough left over for a pan loaf. It's gone up again you know, bread has—halfpenny a loaf. May not be much, but it mounts up. Think of the loaves of bread you can eat in a lifetime. If I'm in good fettle I can go through a loaf a week, that's fifty-two loaves a year. Supposing you live to be a hundred, how many weeks is that?"

"Five thousand two hundred."

"It's a lot, isn't it? I suppose you get used to it. It's the first four thousand weeks that's the worst, but after that you can go on living for ever. People live longer now than they used to, you know. I suppose it's the cold weather. It keeps them fresh. In winter I can buy myself a bit of fish and if I re-member to put it out on the window sill it keeps for a week. Not that I buy much fish in winter. Have you seen the prices? I passed a fish shop today and the herrings were so expensive you'd think they were salmon. It's a Jewish fish you know, herring. Do you have them down your way?"

"Herrings?"

"Jews. We had them up our way, and they hardly ate anything else—barrel-loads. I bet they're eating salmon now. They make it quick, don't they?"

"They make it quick?"

"The Jews do, money. I don't suppose it's got anything to do with eating herrings, because if it did I'd be making it as quick as the rest of them. And if it isn't herrings it's pilchards. I think they're related, pilchards and herrings I mean, cousins or something of that sort. I boil them myself. I boil everything, and then keep the water to make soup. It's surprising the things you can make soup out of. I'm sorry I never keep the recipes. I've had lovely soups, only I never remember what I put into them. Depends on what I've left over, you see. Add a few potatoes, a bit of salt, boil it in water, and you've got soup. I've got some on the boil now if you'd like to try some."

"I would like some very much—"

"Good, I'll—"

"But, as you see, I am trying to study. My exams come in another three weeks and I am not nearly ready."

"Yes, you look busy."

"I have to be: it is only three weeks and I know nothing."

"Ah, you want to meet my friend George, he knows everything. He does, you know, everything. I think it's knowing so much that makes him nasty. You know you can get indigestion in the head the same as indigestion in the stomach, and I don't mind telling you that's when I turn nasty. When I've got indigestion I'm not myself. But I watch it, you see. George doesn't. Reads everything he sets his eyes on, books, papers, railway time-tables—not that he ever goes anywhere. If he spends fourpence on a bus that's him on an excursion. He's a bit tight, George. Not that I'm loose myself, but I don't mind spending a copper if I have to; but him, if he parts with a penny it's like he's parting with an old friend. He's got a few quid salted away I can tell you. He won the premium bonds once, I know that for sure. We were sitting in the library and he was going over the Ernie numbers with a magnifying glass when he gave a sudden loud whoop. We all turned round. 'Anything the matter?' I said. 'No,' he said, 'just my bladder twinging,' but on the way home he bought me a cup of tea and a bun, and when George starts dishing out tea and buns you know that either the Day of Judgement is near, or his ship's come in. You know if I have tea in his place I bring my own buns—I suppose I'm lucky I don't have to bring tea and sugar as well. And when you take sugar you daren't overload your spoon because he's watching you as if you're draining his life's blood. Yes. No good telling him you can't take it with you because he denies he has it in the first place and I suppose none of us like to think we'll be going one day. Funny that, no matter how old you are you think you've got all the time in the world—"

"Well, I haven't. I have so little time, I don't know what to do first. My exams come in three weeks. I haven't even time to take food."

"No time for food?"

"Not a minute."

"I should find time if I was you. No good starving yourself, you know. You don't get work out of a horse if you don't feed him, you don't get work out of yourself if you don't eat. I always—"

"I do. In fact, I was going to sit down to a meal when you came in."

"You mean I'm disturbing you?"

"Well—"

"I mean if you're busy you shouldn't let me stand around chatting here. If you want me to go just tell me to go and I'll go. There's some people just don't know when they're not wanted. Yes. Do you do your own cooking? I do myself. Costs a fortune to eat out, not that I do. But it costs enough to eat in, so I imagine what it's like to eat out. Mind you they say Chinese things aren't expensive, that's on account of Chinamen being so cheap, but I don't know if I could eat their fancy things. Birds I could eat, I suppose. I've eaten pigeon and I suppose one bird is as good as another, but I couldn't eat nests, not birds' nests. You know what birds do in their nests, don't you. Mind you it's surprising what you can eat if you have to. I've a friend—he's dead now—who once ate a camel. That's not why he died though. I don't suppose he ate all of it—had a bit, a leg or breast or something, with rice. It was in the war you see, the first one not this one, and there was nothing else left they could eat. Wonder what they did with the bones? They would have made a lovely soup. I suppose they roasted it over an open fire. Must have done. You could hardly get a camel into a saucepan. A bath would have been big enough, but I shouldn't suppose they had baths out in the desert. They must have been good and hungry though."

"They couldn't have been hungrier than I am."

"What's that?"

"I haven't eaten all day."

"Yes. Looking at you you'd think you haven't eaten for a week. Yes, you'd better learn to look after yourself. There was old Philip. Philip, I don't suppose you've ever heard of him, and in any case he's dead now. Used to forget to eat. If there wasn't anyone around to remind him he'd nearly starve.

Mind you, he saved himself a lot of money that way, starving at his own expense and then getting stocked up in hospital on the National Health. He'd spend half the year in hospital just being fed, and hospital food's good you know. Plenty of greens in winter. Money's no object to these people you know, meat three times a week. Fresh bread every day. Live like lords. That must be in paradise—being in hospital in good health. Yes, there's drawbacks in everything—you find that as you grow older. There's drawbacks in being married, there's drawbacks in staying single. There's drawbacks in being young, there's drawbacks in being old; though speaking as one who's been both I can tell you I'd rather be young. Yes, you live your first twenty years and you live off them for the next sixty. When I was a young fellow, not much older than yourself—" I suddenly noticed that while I was speaking he had begun to undress.

"Feeling hot?" I said.

"No," he said, "going to bed," and pulled a pajama jacket over his vest.

"Here, is it that late?"

"It's very late, and I need to be up early tomorrow."

"Yes, I used to be an early riser myself—still am. At least I wake early, or I used to. Don't seem to now so much. I used to go by Mrs. McConnachie flushing her lavatory at half past six, but when she's away or she's got constipation I don't know where

I am, and she has been away a lot lately, hasn't she? More away than here I'd say. I wonder what she does with herself, not that it's any of my business. But people don't keep coming and going all the time for nothing—apart from anything else it's expensive. Did you see her last time she came back —in a taxi. Mind you she can afford it. She owns this house, and another like it, and she's got all sorts of jobs. She must be worth a penny or two that one. They say she's the wealthiest woman in the street. Of course, that's not saying much. This part of town's had its ups and downs. When I was a lad, I remember they used to have livered coach-men—" he had now taken off his trousers and put on his pajama trousers over his underpants, and before I knew what was happening, he was in bed.

"Good night," he said. "Will you please be good enough to put out the light as you go out."

Funny people, blacks.

A funny thing happened to me today—well I don't know if it was all that funny. It was getting on towards evening and nearly dark. I was sitting in my room doing nothing and thinking what to do next, when I heard the slow creak of footsteps above my head going this way and that, that way and this. Still working for his exams, poor lad, I thought. And he continued to creak on, this way and that, that way and this.

Well, I'm no George, but I do know a thing or two, specially when it comes to English, at least compared to him, and I thought I might be able to help him. So I went upstairs, and there he was with a wet towel round his head, walking up and down, books on his table, books on his bed, papers on the floor, and talking to himself.

"Busy then?" I said.

At first he stood there with his mouth open not saying anything. Then he said, "Busy, very busy,

110

terrifically busy. I have examinations in another few days and the nearer they come the less I remember."

"Yes," I said, "I have a bit of trouble with my memory myself, but you know it's surprising the things I remember. I remember when I was three years old—what am I talking about?—I could hardly have been more than two, or two and a half at most. I was staying with an aunt in Chelmsford. It was just a village then, Chelmsford. The way places grow is fantastic. Of course nothing's been growing quicker than London itself. When I was a boy, half the places that are now in London had never even been heard of. Take Golders Green. Have you heard of Golders Green? No, I'm sure you haven't. I hadn't heard of it neither, and no wonder. It wasn't there, you see. And it's still growing, London is. Soon it'll stretch all the way to Brighton. Hardly worth stretching to, is it? Used to be a pleasure going to Brighton when I was a lad. I was there again two years ago on a British Legion outing. Couldn't wait to come back. Tar on the beaches and hooligans in the street—and on the beaches too, they and their girl friends. The things we saw, even though we weren't looking. I was glad there were no ladies in our party I can tell you. I'm not saying people didn't do those things in my day, but this was all out in the open, in broad daylight, on the beach. The police didn't lift a finger to stop it. The trouble is,

111

you see, policemen are hardly more than lads themselves. They'd probably do the same if they had half the chance. George's cousin is a policeman, or was in the war—special constable. He lost something in the war, I can't remember now what it was, but he got a medal for it. But whatever it was he managed well without it. He died only last year —no, it must have been two years ago. Two and a half years ago. It was mid-summer. He was sitting on a park bench having a smoke when he was suddenly switched off. His pipe was still going when they found him. That's the best way to go, you know, like someone creeping up on you unexpected. There's many a time I wake up in the morning, or after a doze in the afternoon, and I think, ah yes, this is it, I've snuffed it. Do you ever get that feeling? Well you will when you're a bit older. Ah yes, I think, I've snuffed, but there I've been alive all along.

"You know what I sometimes think? I sometimes think being dead is only in the eye of the beholder—you know, like being beautiful. Do you see what I mean? You don't? Well, for example, for all I know I might be dead now, only this is my spirit hanging on out of habit—only I don't know about it, you see? You know, like Charles, King Charles the one with the head off. Well, they say after he lost his head he kept talking for some minutes, not knowing he was dead. Well if you can speak with your head off, there's no knowing what you can do with your head on—did you want to say something?"

"No, nothing. Just if you wouldn't mind excusing me. I have examinations soon and I am going out of my head."

"Examinations you said?"

"Yes, and I am going out of my head."

"No, that won't do, will it? You want to be right inside your head if you have examinations. Yes. I never had much of an education myself—not many people did when I was a lad, but I do read, at least I did when my eyes were better, and I still read now—though not as much as I used to. But I still believe in them you know, I do, I believe in books. No library should be without them. Have you tried it? You ought to try it. A very fine library, just down the road, and full of colored gentlemen like yourself."

I stopped talking, for he was beginning to undress again, just like the night before, and he wasn't shy either, first his shirt, then his trousers, and before I knew what was happening he had nothing on but a thick, woolen vest, and droopy underpants.

"Feeling hot?" I said.

"No, not hot. Tired, very tired. I'm going to bed. Would you mind putting out the light as you go out?"

And he dived into bed and buried himself under the blankets.

113

A bit later I was sitting down sipping a cup of tea, when it occurred to me that perhaps the fellow wasn't well. Diving into bed like that at six in the evening, no healthy person does that. Perhaps he had one of those Asiatic things like the black death, or small-pox or foot and mouth disease. You don't hear much of it nowadays. I've heard of people having about everything—but not the black death. I suppose it's something the blacks catch. I hope it's not catching. British plagues are enough to get on with for me.

And as I was pouring myself out a second cup, I thought the poor fellow could do with a cup, lying up there sick, miles from home, with no one to talk to. So I rinsed out the teapot, brewed some fresh tea, and went upstairs on tiptoe with the saucer over the cup so as it shouldn't get cold.

I knocked on the door very gently. He couldn't have heard, so I knocked louder.

"Who's that?" he said.

"Me," I said, and went in.

Instead of lying in bed, he was sitting up by his table, in a dressing-gown, writing. I don't know what happened next, but he suddenly gave a scream as if he'd been stabbed, leapt right across the room, and almost slammed the door in my face. The cup and saucer went flying out of my hand.

I stood outside the door not knowing whether to call the police or a doctor. And while I stood there the door opened and he came out. I had no idea what he wanted, but I took no chances. I clattered down the stairs as fast as I could, into my room, locked the door, pushed my bed against it, and almost collapsed on top of it.

I was lying there, puffing with my hand to my side to keep down an ache, when there was a knock on the door. I sat up and looked around for a weapon. There was nothing but an earthenware cat on the mantelpiece. I grabbed that.

"This is Sayed," he said.

"Go away," I shouted. "Go away."

"I am sorry, I was upset. I am terribly sorry."

"Go away."

"I have been sleeping badly and I am upset. I am terribly sorry."

"Go away. Go back to India."

With that he said nothing more. I put my ear against the door and heard him shuffle slowly up the stairs, and then pick up the remains of the cup and saucer on the landing. I waited till I could hear his door shut, before I put the cat back on the mantelpiece and got back onto the bed.

I was wakened by the door bell.

It was George. I hardly recognized him. There had never been much of him, but he had shrunk into almost nothing. His face was white and wrinkled like a raisin, and there was dust in the wrinkles.

"I was passing this way," he said, "so I thought I'd look in and see how you were. I don't suppose you've been able to get out much with your bad leg."

"No," I said, "not much."

"No, nor me neither. Fog's worse than anything, worse than snow or ice or rain. Haven't been able to tell whether it's day or night."

"No, nor me neither."

He looked around him at the street. "It's clearing up a bit though."

"Yes," I said, "a bit."

And he said nothing and I said nothing.

116

Then he said, "It's Wednesday today, isn't it?"

"Wednesday is it?"

"Must be, yesterday was Tuesday."

"Yes, then it must be."

"And it's nearly three o'clock."

"Three?"

"In the afternoon."

"It can't be."

"It is."

"I only just got up. Not three in the afternoon, it can't be."

"It is. And look, I brought some buns along for Choral Evensong."

"I haven't made my bed."

"I'll help you make it."

"The heater isn't working."

"I'll fix it."

And he almost squeezed past me to get up the stairs.

He fixed the heater, we made the bed, had tea and listened to Choral Evensong, but it wasn't quite like old times. All the time I was listening to the singing and sipping tea I kept wondering why it wasn't, and George looked as if he was wondering himself, sunk there, low in the chair, with his shoulders hunched up and both hands round his tea-cup. He hardly said anything and made a quiet noise, a cross between a gasp and a grunt.

When the program was over I said to him, "I've been having trouble."

117

"Trouble?"

"Him upstairs."

"Him upstairs?"

"The black fellow."

"The black fellow?" At this he came to life. "I forgot all about him. Been giving you trouble, has he? I said he would, didn't I? I told you that from the beginning. They're trouble wherever they go. What sort of trouble?"

"Wait and I'll tell you."

"A woman in our street's had trouble with them. Oh, I knew he'd be trouble as soon as I saw him. Yes. Been giving you trouble, has he. What sort of trouble?"

"I'm trying to tell you. Last night. It was terrible last night, cold and foggy, and I went upstairs to give him a cup of tea, when—"

"Give him a cup of tea? The black fellow?"

"Yes."

"What did you want to do that for?"

"He wasn't feeling well, so I thought I'd make him a nice cup of tea. So I made him a cup and went upstairs, and what do you think happened?"

"An orgy."

"A what?"

"You found him in bed with two women."

"What would he be doing in bed with two women?"

"The same as he'd be doing in bed with one woman. They go in for that sort of thing."

118

"Well he wasn't in bed with two women. He wasn't even in bed with one woman. He wasn't even in bed. He was just reading, looking quite peaceful, but as soon as I opened the door he gave a wild scream and jumped on me. I ran down the stairs and he came after me. I just got here in time, locked the door, and jammed the bed against it."

"Yes. I'm surprised it didn't happen earlier. A case of reversion to primeval instincts."

"A case of what?"

"Of reversion to primeval instincts."

"I thought it was something like that."

"You've got to remember these people are only a step away from the jungle. That fellow's father was probably a cannibal eating missionaries the same as you and me eat pilchards. Not that I blame them. I mean cannibals have to eat something and anyone who tried to peddle God round the jungles deserves to be eaten. But that doesn't mean we've got to have these people living on top of us."

"He's not the man-eating type, that one upstairs. He doesn't look as if he eats anything at all. He's more skin and bone than anything else."

"Yes, I don't suppose a normal diet agrees with him. And there's the sex you see, that keeps people thin."

"Sex?"

"Sex."

"That's what I thought you said. You can't get away from it these days, can you?"

119

"That's not surprising because sex is at the bottom of everything. You've read Freud haven't you?"

"Yes, who hasn't read Freud. Very true what he says."

"Very true. And you see it's all a matter of calories."

"Yes, I suppose it must be."

"I was reading about it in the Reader's Digest the other day. Being thin or fat depends on the balance between the calories you take in and the calories you spend. Now you take in calories when you eat—"

"And you spend calories when you shit."

"No, that you don't do. That's a very economic activity. Hardly costs you any calories at all, unless you're badly constipated, that is, but normally passing your food costs you nothing. No, it's walking that uses up calories, running, climbing, physical activity of all sorts. Now I read in the Reader's Digest that on the average sleeping with a woman uses up the same amount of calories as running a mile."

"Same as running a mile."

"On the average."

"That's why you get all these fellows chasing across the country. I was always wondering why they did it."

"No, I don't think you've got me right, Cyril."

"I used to do a bit of running myself when I was younger, but I must say—"

"No, Cyril, you haven't got me right. What I mean is these black people often look thin because of all the sex they have. It's the sex that keeps them thin."

"The sex?"

"Yes, you see, because of the calories they use up. It keeps them thin."

"I must tell that to Mrs. McConnachie, she's always complaining about her weight. But do you mean all the thin people you see are thin because of sex? I mean you're not too fat yourself, George?"

"Yes, but I've got a high metabolism."

"A high metabolism?"

"Always have had."

"I see."

"And I've lived an energetic life. Been very active always."

"Maybe he has, too. He's coming and going all the time, rushing here and there and everywhere. But I've never seen him out with a woman."

"It's not the outs that count, it's the ins."

"I've never seen him in with a woman either."

"Not once?"

"Not once."

"He's probably one of the sly types. They're the worst of the lot."

And even as he was speaking I could hear the black fellow shuffle past my door on the way to the lavatory. He walked like an old man. He even murmured to himself like an old man.

121

Mrs. McConnachie came back today.

"Anyone at home?" she shouted, and when I went out, there she was on the landing in a brand-new fur coat looking like a cross between a chinchilla and a cow. She was holding up a small package in her hand.

"I've got a present for you."

I unwrapped it. It was a hairy little potted plant.

"Company for George's Elasticus Fisticus," she said. "But don't keep them too near together. It's a sexy little thing." She was looking at my face as she was speaking to me.

"Are you all right?" she said.

"I'm fine."

"Been ill?"

"Never felt better."

"I don't like the way you look. You're gray as slush and all dusty. Have you been looking after yourself?"

122

"Looking after myself?"

"Have you been looking after yourself?"

"I've hardly been doing anything else."

"Well I don't like the way you look."

I was going to say "you're no picture yourself," but that's not the sort of thing you say to a lady.

"You've been skimping, haven't you?" she said.

"Skimping?"

"Don't look at me as if you've never heard the word. Skimping. Have you been feeding yourself properly?"

"Course I have."

"Course you have. Bread and pilchards, soup out of the left-overs, and weak tea. You needn't tell me what you've been feeding yourself on. What are you saving for? Old age? To leave it all to the R.S. P.C.A. when you snuff it, so that you can have your name in the papers? I don't know what it is between old people and animals. I once knew an old woman who kept fourteen cats in clover, and starved herself to death."

"Well I'm not starving myself to death."

"No, if your diets are anything to go by, you're feeding yourself to death. Well, what are you saving for, tell me, what are you saving for?"

"I'm not saving."

"You're not saving?"

"I'm not saving."

"I've seen you in the post office, collecting your

123

pension in one counter and paying into the savings bank at the other."

"That was for my Christmas club."

"Your what?"

"My Christmas club."

"I saw the Christmas do you and George had. Meat pies and tea."

"And crackers."

"And crackers."

"Turkeys don't agree with me."

"No, but I'm sure you'd have bought a couple if they did. If you want to keep the post office going that's your business, but it's me that's subsidizing you. I'm charging you thirty bob a week for the room, fully furnished. I could get three for it at least. Old Dora charges four. Well, mate, new terms from tomorrow. You either spend ten bob more a week on food, or the rent goes up to two quid."

"Ten bob did you say?"

"Ten shillings."

"I haven't got another ten bob."

"Haven't you?"

"I haven't."

"Well I happen to be friendly with a gentleman who's clerk in your old firm and I know what you're getting a week from them. It's not a fortune, but it's enough to get you a half a cabbage now and again, and even a lettuce on your birthday."

"All right," I said, "another five bob."

"Don't argue with me as if you're doing me favors, mate. It's your own miserable face you'll be spending the money on. Ten bob on food or ten bob on the rent."

She then took me down to the bathroom and weighed me.

"I'll be weighing you again next week," she said, "and if there's no difference, up goes the rent."

"I've got a high metabolism," I said.

"Well then, you'd better get yourself a low one."

Later in the evening I was clearing up after supper when I heard her shout on the stairs.

"Cyril are you up there?"

"Yes."

"Well come down here."

I hung up my dish-cloth, washed my hands, and went down.

Mrs. M was in her living-room with her friend Dora, and wearing her fur coat.

"Cyril, we need a man's opinion. What do you think of my coat?"

"I think it's lovely, Flora," said Dora, "I really do."

"Looks good and warm," I said.

"It does something for you, Flora," said Dora.

"Doesn't it make me look big?"

I said nothing, neither did Dora.

"Well, doesn't it?" She looked from Dora to me and from me to Dora.

"Depends how you look at it," I said.

"Supposing you look at it with your eyes open?"

"Yes," I said, "it's a lovely coat."

"It is lovely, Flora."

"I took a fancy to it as soon as I saw it. That's me, I said, but now that I'm wearing it I feel like somebody else. Makes me feel like a kept woman— wish I was."

"The hairs stand up a bit though," I said.

"That's passion, Cyril old man. Your hair would also stand on end if I had you as close."

At this Dora threw back her head and laughed till her bosom looked as if it might jump out of her blouse. She had a thick neck like Mrs. M but it was soft and white. Mrs. M's was gnarled and red.

"Well, do you like it?" said Mrs. M.

"I said I did."

"You're not saying it just because you want to get back to The Archers?"

"No, I like it."

"You like it?"

"I like it."

"Are you sure you like it?"

"I'm sure I like it, only—"

"Only what?"

"Won't it be a bit cold round the knees?"

"You mean it's too short?"

"Just around the knees."

"It's meant to be," said Dora. "I've had my skirts raised."

126

"I'll bet you have," said Mrs. M, and she broke into a cackle. She stopped when she saw me, and I suddenly felt as if I shouldn't be there.

"You shouldn't talk like that when Cyril's about," said Dora. "He's a gentleman."

"At his age he might as well be," said Mrs. M, and began cackling again. "Give me another year or two, Dora dear, and I'll be a lady."

I was kept awake for half the night by a raging wind which kept whooping in the chimney and rattling my windows. By early morning it was so wild that I was half afraid the house would come down.

"March has come in like a lion," said George when he called on me. I was surprised the wind hadn't bowled him over.

We went down to the library, arm in arm, him using me as an anchor, bent almost double against the wind.

"Well the winter's over, that's for sure," said George. "We'll be able to make the park tomorrow."

"If it blows like this," I said, "we should be able to fly there." The snow had disappeared overnight, but the streets were muddy and slippery, and once or twice we nearly went down together. The longer we walked the farther the library seemed to get. The sky was a powder-gray, with small, white

128

clouds bounding across it, and the buildings, the
trees, and the lamp-posts stood out as if someone
had gone over their outlines with a black pencil.

"I've left my heater on," I suddenly remember,
"shouldn't I get back to put it off?"

"What? We're nearly there. I'd leave it on, it's
not that warm yet."

"But it uses up a lot of paraffin. This one uses
more paraffin than the last one did, although it's
half the size."

"It shouldn't do."

"It's no good saying it shouldn't do if it does."

"It wouldn't do if it was used properly."

We stopped, and I took my arm out of his.

"Are you saying I don't even know how to work
a bleeding paraffin heater?"

"I'm not saying you can't work it properly. I'm
saying that if you did work it properly it wouldn't
be using up so much paraffin."

"It's not using up much paraffin, only the other
one used up less."

"Then what are you worried about?"

"I'm not worrying about anything, but I don't
like waste."

"A warm room isn't waste."

"It is if it's warm anyway."

"Who says it's warm?"

"I say it's warm."

"Then if it's warm why did you leave the heater
on?"

"Is it your heater or mine?"

"It's—"

"Is it your heater or mine?"

"It's—"

"Just you answer me. Is it your heater or mine?"

"If you'll give me a chance I will."

"Is it your heater or mine?"

"As a matter of fact it's mine, only I happened to lend it to you—if you remember."

"You did?"

"It doesn't matter. I don't need it back. It's an old one I had, but seeing you asked, I told you."

He sniggered to himself after that, all the way to the library.

We didn't have much to say to each other and all the time we were in the library, he was bent over the papers with a smirk on his face, raising one eye every now and again to have a glance at me. I left him sitting there after a bit, and went to a café and bought myself a slap-up meal, oxtail soup, pie and chips, jam-tart and custard and tea. I had a table by the window and as he was going home he saw me there.

"Won the pools?" he said, looking closely at the jam-tart floating on a lake of custard.

I called over the boy. "Give this man a cup of tea and put it on my bill."

George looked at me as if he couldn't believe his ears.

"Have you?" he said. "Have you won the pools?"

"No," I said, "this is Be-Good-to-Cyril week. Nobody else is much good to Cyril, so I thought I'd better be."

"I wouldn't mind being good to George if I could afford it," he said, "but I can't."

"Can't you?"

"Of course I can't. This little lot must have put you back a good three bob."

"Four and a tanner," I said, "including your cup of tea."

"There you are, who can afford money like that?"

"You can for one."

"I can?"

"If I can you can. I bet you've got a few bob salted away."

"What makes you think I have?"

"I know you have. I can see it by the way you shy away to a corner of the library table to have a good look at your post office savings book. It's your favorite reading. And I've seen you in the post office, collecting your pension at one counter, and paying it back at the other."

"That's to cover my obligations." He looked at the cup of tea which the boy had brought him a little uncertainly. "It's all right," I said, "drink it. I'm paying for it."

He put both his hands round it and sipped it, looking at me over the rim.

"I've been thinking things out," I said, "and I've been thinking, we don't live forever."

131

"How long did it take you to work that out?"

"I was thinking it out in bed last night, and I was thinking, why worry about tomorrow, tomorrow may never come—in fact the older you get the better the chance that it won't, and I thought I had better be good to myself while I can still enjoy it."

"You're quite right, if you can afford it."

"If I can afford it, you can."

"I've got obligations."

"Obligations?"

"I've got obligations."

"Such as your Ficus elastica?"

"Such as my funeral expenses."

"Your funeral expenses?"

"Yes."

"And I suppose when I snuff it they'll feed me to the pigeons?"

"That's your funeral, not mine. I want a decent burial."

"I've been paying up two and four a month to a burial society for the last forty-seven years, and I'll put my burial against yours any day of the week."

"I've been paying two and nine a month."

"But I've been paying longer."

"You haven't, you know."

"I have, you know."

"What are you getting for yours?"

"Oak coffin, brass handles—and a four-foot stone."

"Ha. I'm getting a six-foot stone."

"Six foot?"

"In granite."

"Well, if you want to be extravagant you can be."

"Extravagant?"

"A six-foot stone is extravagant."

"Well, if you're getting yourself a four-footer, I'd look silly with anything less than six, wouldn't I? I'm half as big as you again aren't I? And I'm laying on transport for my friends—that shouldn't come to much now."

"No," he said quietly.

"Do you remember when Dick died?"

"Poor Dick."

"There was a whole line of cars—a fleet of limousines."

"No, not a fleet, Cyril. The hearse, and three behind. I remember counting them."

"Well there was only one car for poor Harry."

"Yes, and by the time I'll go you won't even need one. You'll be able to ride in front with the undertaker."

"Me in front of the undertaker? I'll snuff it before you I can tell you that much."

"I'll bet you you won't."

"I'll bet you I will."

"The way I've been feeling lately I'm ready to go any time."

"And do you think I've been feeling much better?"

133

"Yes, but you're bothered by your externals. My trouble is internal, and internal trouble is more serious."

"It's not more serious than my external ones, I can tell you that much."

"And I've been breathing badly."

"There's been times of the night when I haven't been breathing at all."

"I'll be going first, I can feel it in my bones."

"That's the rheumatics."

"We'll see."

"We'll see."

And when he ordered another cup of tea for which he paid himself, I really believed him.

We thought we'd make a break for the park, but it's still stormy and we made it only as far as the library, and stopped there for the morning.

As I was going home, bent against the wind, a fire engine roared past me, and then a second, and then a third. And behind it came an ambulance and behind the ambulance a police car, all of them clanging bells, flashing lights and kicking up dust. I hadn't seen anything like it since the war.

I went after them as fast as I could, which was not very fast, and soon came to a road which was blocked by the police, with a large crowd gathered behind a barrier, and the whole roadway wet and strewn with hoses. The fire was out, but the building was smoldering and the firemen were still playing hoses on it.

"Anyone hurt?" I asked a fellow next to me.

"No, only a darkie. He jumped from the top window—panicked."

135

It was only then that it struck me that the smoldering building was my house—or at least Mrs. McConnachie's.

I suddenly felt giddy and must have passed out. I remember thinking even as I was falling: I told George I'd snuff it first, and when I came to I was a bit disappointed. I was sitting up in bed with Mrs. M by my side (not in the bed though).

"So you're alive then," she said, "or are you?"

I looked at her and round me trying to make out where I was.

"There's been a fire," I said.

"You're not kidding, are you. I thought you'd gone up in smoke yourself. Your paraffin heater caught fire."

"The black fellow," I suddenly remembered. "He's all right, isn't he?"

"Would you be all right if you'd jumped from the top floor?"

"Is he—"

"He's alive, but only just and with things broken right and left. Some poor buggers can never raise their heads without being slapped down. The less you have in life the more you're likely to lose it."

George came in to see me a bit later.

"You're all right then?"

"Just about."

"You weren't when I came earlier. You looked as if you were gone for good."

"It was the shock."

"Must have been."

"Did you hear about the black fellow?"

"Yes, disgraceful, wasn't it. That's what I meant when I said it's dangerous to have these people on top of you. They panic at the slightest thing. There wasn't much of a fire at all—just your old paraffin stove going up in flames and setting fire to the curtains. As soon as he saw the flames he jumped —didn't even try the staircase."

"He was badly hurt, was he?"

"They say he broke a thing or two," We sat quietly for a bit, then he said, "And what's going to happen to you?"

"Me?"

"Where are you going to live? It'll be a day or two before you'll be able to use your room again."

And it was then that I realized I was sitting up in Mrs. McConnachie's bed in her kitchen alcove.

"That's where she sleeps," he said, "isn't it?"

"Yes."

"Exactly, and you've got to watch it with her."

"What do you mean?"

"What do I mean?"

"What do you mean?"

"She's got a reputation, that's what I mean."

"A reputation?"

"A reputation."

"What sort of reputation?"

"When you hear of somebody having a reputation there's only one sort of reputation they can

137

have. You know she's lost her job as school-crossing attendant, don't you?"

"No, I didn't."

"So you won't know why she lost it."

"I still don't know what you're talking about."

"It was because some mothers complained that she wasn't morally fit to lead their children across the road, that's why she lost it."

"What's she done?"

"She's a woman of easy virtue."

"Easy virtue?"

"She's a woman of easy virtue."

"And do you know any women of difficult virtue?"

"Cyril, you're tired, you're not well. It's no good speaking to you about a delicate matter."

"You can't start blaspheming a poor old woman just like that without saying what you mean."

"I said what I mean, only you don't understand what I said. She carries on, she's been carrying on with a man ten years younger than her."

"Has she?"

"With a fellow ten years younger than her."

"Where did you hear all this?"

"I heard."

"Where?"

"You're forgetting I had a sister."

"But she's been dead ten years."

"This all happened ten years ago."

"That doesn't count. If you'd robbed a bank ten years ago they couldn't touch you for it."

"But we're not talking about banks, we're talking about morals. That woman hasn't got any."

"Morals?"

"Morals. She'll come to a sticky end that one."

"All ends are sticky."

"But hers'll be stickier than most, you'll see. Apart from anything else she's masquerading under a false pretension."

"What do you mean?"

"She calls herself Mrs. McConnachie, doesn't she?"

"So what?"

"Have you ever seen Mr. McConnachie?"

"No."

"Have you ever heard of him?"

"No."

"Does she ever mention him?"

"No."

"Exactly."

"What's that supposed to prove?"

"She's trying to pass herself as a respectable, widowed woman. Whereas she's neither respectable nor widowed. And then there's her friend Dora. You've heard about Dora, haven't you?"

"No."

"Then you've seen her, and if you've seen her that's enough."

Mrs. M returned while we were talking and George at once changed the subject to last month's Balance of Trade figures, about which he knows a great deal.

139

She seemed good and merry.

"Hullo, George," she said, "and how is your fucking elastic?"

"My Ficus elastica, you mean?"

"That's what I meant. I know it had something to do with rubber."

"It's very well, thank you. I was just asking Cyril where he's going to stay while his room's being repaired."

"Right here. It's a big bed," she said and winked at me. "That fire was no accident. I had it all fixed so as to get Cyril into my bed."

"I think I'd better be going," said George, "I've forgotten to water my plant."

"Water it well," she shouted after him, "and if you need any help don't hesitate to call on me."

She then turned her attention to me and sat there, with one eye closed against her cigarette, and the other one gleaming, and I didn't know whether to sit upright or to sink under the blankets.

"Have you seen George's Ficus elastica?" I said.

"No."

"It's big."

"Is it?"

"Bigger than George himself."

"Fancy."

And she remained there, legs wide apart, hands clasped over her stomach, one eye shut, the other beaming.

"He used to have a cat."

"Did he?"

"It died though. He had it stuffed, but it got so full of worms that it began moving all over again, and he had to have it put away."

"Fancy."

And she sat there with her fag still smoldering. I looked up at the ceiling.

"The ceiling's beginning to peel."

"Beginning to peel, is it?"

"The paint's flaking."

"Flaking, is it?"

"It is."

"I'd better do something about it, hadn't I?"

"It'll get worse if you don't."

"But not tonight"—and she took off her glasses.

At that moment the phone rang and I sank underneath my blankets. She came back a minute later looking sad, worried and old. She always looked sad and old without her glasses—as if all her heartiness and cheer were in them—but what's worrying her?

George called on me early this morning and looked at me closely when I opened the door.

"Well?" he said. It was a long, drawn-out 'well.'

"Well what?"

"What happened last night?"

"Last night?"

"What happened?"

"Why. What should have happened?"

He looked around him and lowered his voice. "Did she molest you?"

"Molest me?"

"Did she get into bed with you?" he almost shouted. And then I suddenly understood what he was talking about.

"No, she didn't get into bed with me, at least not that I know of." I nudged him in the ribs. "Here, you don't think she got at me while I was asleep?"

"I'd put nothing past her," said George. "You heard the way she spoke."

142

"She speaks like that all the time."

"So you know what I mean."

"I don't know what you mean."

"Foul mouth, foul morals."

"Falmouth what?"

"Foul mouth," he said, "foul morals. It's an old proverb."

"The more said, the less done," I said. "That's an old proverb. I don't know where you get all this talk about morals all of a sudden. I've never heard you talk about them before. What are you doing with morals at your age?"

"I've had time to think—those three days in the fog. Fog is very good for thinking, and it occurred to me then that there's something in morals. People are like indoor plants you know. You not only have to water them, you have to dust them. What dust is to the Ficus elastica, immorality is to human beings. If you let the dust pile up—they die."

In the afternoon I went to visit the black fellow in hospital. He was covered from shoulders to feet in bandages, with splints here and there, and head lolling limply on the pillow.

"I'm glad to see you looking so well," I said.

He nodded wearily.

"Yes," I said, "you're looking fine."

He didn't say anything but kept nodding his head to the side as if trying to shake water out of his ear.

"They're very good at breakages here," I told

him, "you know, at putting pieces together. They're not much good at anything else but they are good at that. They treated a friend of mine for a broken head a week or two before he died, marvelous job they made of it. It's the soft parts you've got to worry about—hearts, lungs and thinks like that, bladder too, that's George's trouble. You don't know George, do you? No, I didn't think you did. He takes a bit of knowing, George. He came back from the war—the first one that is——with bits of daylight showing through him and he's not been able to smile since. He can snigger though, and smirk, but not smile, or laugh out loud. I'm not saying he doesn't find things funny. He does, at least I think he does, only it doesn't show on his face. Not like Mrs. McConnachie. It shows all over with her, doesn't it, her face, her—especially when she's wearing a tight dress. You always expect something to come apart when she's having a good giggle. Once it did, buttons flying all over the place and ricocheting round the room like bullets. A friend of mine, an old soldier, who was with us at the time, said it was like being in the front line all over again. Mind you, it's her own jokes mostly which does it. There's a few she knows that I would never tell in public, at least not in mixed company. Shall I tell you one? It makes me laugh every time I think of it. You see there was this black fellow and he—no, not a good one that. Have you heard the one about the school-teacher? Well there was this school-teacher—you've heard it?"

144

He was nodding his head to the side and I wasn't
sure if he was nodding to say yes, nodding in his
sleep, or just having a quiet fit.

"He's not what you'd call a picture of health, is
he?" said Mrs. M when I got back. "Poor boy. It's
not only his breakages, it's his exams. He'll never
be able to sit them now, not this year, and he was
working so hard, all day and all night. It'll keep him
in hospital for weeks. You're always slow to mend
with worries on your head." She sat silently with a
hand on each knee looking out of the window. It
was a bright, cold afternoon. "One way or the other
I haven't had much luck. You get used to that, but
I think I must be unlucky to others. There's not a
soul who's stayed in this house who hasn't been
unlucky." She turned to me.

"Do you believe in fate?"

"Fate?"

"Do you believe in luck? I mean take the number
of the street to begin with—a hundred and sixty-
nine. Does it mean anything to you?"

"A hundred and sixty-nine?"

"Does it mean anything to you?"

"Nothing that I can think of."

"Then it doesn't matter. It didn't to me either,
but then a few years ago a fellow came here to look
for a room. He liked the room all right but as soon
as he saw the number he almost jumped in the air
and ran for it."

"What's so special about the number?"

"It's thirteen times thirteen: you couldn't be

145

unluckier than that. Perhaps you should change your lodgings, Cyril."

"Change my what?"

"Your lodgings."

"What for? I've been as happy here as I have anywhere, in fact happier. All my bad troubles were at my other place."

"What number was that?"

"Seventy-eight."

"There you are. Six times thirteen: it all works out."

"But I wasn't there all that long. I've been around all over."

"Do you remember any of the numbers?"

"There was eighty-seven."

"Eighty-seven you said?"

"Yes."

"There you are. What's eighty-seven from a hundred?"

"Eighty-seven from a hundred?"

"Thirteen. You can't escape it. Poor Sayed is twenty-six. He left Pakistan on January 13th and arrived here on February 13th. He's in a cage of thirteens. No, poor boy, I don't give him much chance."

In the evening I phoned the hospital.

"They say he's as well as can be expected," I told her.

"That doesn't mean anything," she said. "He could be dead and still be as well as could be expected."

When we came to visit him in the evening he had been moved to a small side ward.

"You had better not bother him now," said the nurse.

"He's still alive?" said Mrs. M.

"He's as well as can be expected."

"As well as can be expected," she kept murmuring to herself as we walked home.

We were almost home when she turned to me and said, "Are you a religious man?"

"Religious?"

"Do you believe in God?"

"Yes, I suppose I do, though I don't know if He believes in me."

"I don't believe in anything, only if I knew a prayer I'd say it now. Don't you know any prayers?"

"No, not off-hand."

"What, not with all that listening to the radio, and the prologues and epilogues and the Sunday morning services, and Sunday Half Hour, and

Choral Evensong, and Five to Ten, and Lift up your Arse. You mean to say you don't know one miserly prayer?"

"I know the Lord's prayer."

"Lord who?"

"You know, Our Father, Which Art—"

"That doesn't count—at least it's not the sort of prayer I want."

"It's the only one I know."

"Then we'll have to make one up."

We were just by a pub at the time and she pulled me inside and we sat down to work out a prayer. It wasn't easy, not even after she'd had a couple of large gins and I a pint of beer.

"They all start with 'O God,' don't they?" she said.

"Some of them. Some of them start with 'O Lord.' "

"Then let's begin with 'O Lord God.' "

That was as far as we got until she'd had another gin, and after that it all went in a gush, the whole prayer. She read it out to me:

"O Lord God. You haven't heard much from me lately, but I've never wanted much from you—and a fat chance I would have had of getting it even if I'd wanted it. But as I haven't bothered you much" —and she stopped for another drink and to light up—"but as I haven't bothered you much, I hope you'll have the patience to listen to this. I know I'm not one of your regulars, but this is on behalf

of a lodger who looks as if he may be. He's not
C of E I think, but I don't suppose that matters to
you. Please Lord God spare Sayed, a poor, innocent,
friendless soul. I'm not asking you to do much for
him—just get him out of the mess you got him
into.

"Yours,
"Flora McConnachie (Mrs.)."

"How did that sound?" she asked.

"Not like the prayers they have on the wireless."

"Not Lift up your Arse stuff?"

"Nothing like it."

"But I think He'll understand. He wouldn't be
much of a God if He didn't."

George came round in the evening looking very
peevish.

"I called round for you earlier in the day," he
said. "You weren't in. We could have gone to the
park, you know. No wind, no rain, the weather
almost warm. We could have had an hour in the
park before they closed, but you weren't in."

"The park?—in the evening?"

"It wasn't evening. It was late afternoon."

"But we always go in the morning."

"We do normally. But the weather's been so
bad, storms, fog, snow, coming one after the other,
and sometimes all at once, that I thought we should
take the chance while we have it. But you weren't
in."

"I know. I was out."

149

"I know you were out, but where were you?"

"Where was I?"

"Where were you?"

"Mind your own bleeding business."

"All right, if you want to be like that, be like that. But something's got into you, Cyril. I don't know what it is, and I'm not going to try and find out. But something's got into you. It may be the long winter, I don't know what it is. There's many a time when old Harry used to say to me, 'There goes the kindliest fellow I know,' and I agreed with him. I wonder what poor Harry would think of you if he knew you now."

"It's not me that's changed, George, it's you."

"I've changed?"

"You have. I mean you can't come up to me demanding to know where I've been. We're friends, George, we're not man and wife, and even Elsie when she was alive didn't ask questions like that."

"I was disappointed, that's all. You and me have been talking about a walk in the park all winter. And I came up here all the way specially—I mean the park's up my way, not up yours—and I came up here all the way specially—"

"I didn't know you were coming."

"But you're never out at that time of day normally."

"Well I was this time. I went to visit a friend in hospital."

"The black fellow?"

"The black fellow."

"I thought you were. You seem to have more time for him than for me."

"He's all by himself, thousands of miles from home, and sick."

"As a matter of fact I haven't been too well myself."

"But you haven't jumped from a top-floor window."

"Maybe I should have done. You get no attention without dramatics nowadays. If you're perishing slowly you're left to perish."

"Who's perishing?"

"I am."

"You've been perishing for as long as I've known you."

"You won't have much longer to wait. And when it comes to Choral Evensong I hope the black fellow remembers to bring his buns the same as I did."

And before I could stop him he was out of the room and down the stairs, moving faster than I've heard him move for a long time.

"Will you be calling for me tomorrow then?" I shouted after him.

He didn't answer.

151

A perfect day for the park. I rose early, dressed early and waited for George, knowing full well he wouldn't come. I could see by last night that he was in one of his moods, and if he gets into one of his moods it takes him three weeks to a month to get out of it, and even then he gets out of it grudgingly, as if he's left something precious behind.

When it was half past ten and he still hadn't turned up, I put on my coat and went to call on him.

He was sitting in his front room, deep in his armchair with his greatcoat on and collar about his ears, and speechless.

"Anything wrong, George?" I said, and felt silly, for I had the feeling that something was.

He pointed a quivering finger to the other end of the room. It was the Ficus elasticus, all six foot of it, flat on its face.

152

I didn't know what to say and just sat there saying nothing. After a while he found his voice.

"Died during the night," he said. "It was the fog that did it. It began to droop during the fog. And I watered it and dusted it, and even called in a fellow from the flower shop—but there was nothing I could do to save it. Nearly six foot it was, do you remember, Cyril, it almost touched the ceiling."

"I remember. The finest Ficus elasticus I've seen. But you never mentioned this before. You hadn't said anything about it not being well."

"I don't like troubling people with my worries."

"I knew something was troubling you. When you came up yesterday I could see by your face something was."

"Yes, I could tell then it wouldn't last the night. I couldn't sit in by myself watching it perish, that's why I came to see you, you know, just to have a word. It was a lovely thing."

"The finest I've seen."

"It would have reached the ceiling in another month or two, you know, and did you see the leaves, fine glossy texture. They glowed—you could almost see them in the dark. You know I would sometimes sit in my room in the evening with the lights out, just watching them glisten. It was like a living companion. It's gone."

"Nothing lives forever, you know that, George."

"It had years of life in it yet. In fact I had made arrangements in my will for somebody to look after it. It had years of life in it. It was the fog that did it. It nearly did me too, I wish it had done."

"Now, now, George. You shouldn't upset yourself. You'll get another one."

"No, that I won't, not another. I'm too old to start again, and even if I wasn't I would never be able to find another plant like it. Did you see how deep green the leaves were, and how fat and spongy? Beautiful."

"It was beautiful, but you've got to look at it this way, George. You've had this rubber-plant for four years—"

"Five nearly."

"There's some people who have gone right through life without having a plant at all. You've got to count your blessings."

"Count my blessings?"

"Yes, George. There's the five happy years you've had together. And there's other things you have that others haven't. You're still moving around on your own steam—think of all the fellows we know who aren't."

"Such as who?"

"Such as—they're not even moving about at all. You're still alive, that's something, isn't it? And you may have a bad bladder and war wounds here and there, but you've got more parts in working order than not. Then there's your friends, that's still something. There are people who go around without a friend, in the world, George. You've got friends."

154

"More below ground than above."

"But it's something to have had them in the first place. And then there's your knowledge."

"Yes, there is that," and he sighed, "but I haven't done much with it. For a fellow of my ability I haven't gone far. I could have been a school-master or something, a librarian, but I was never more than a clerk, you know, and not a very high clerk at that. There's people with half my knowledge giving lectures, talking on the radio—I heard a man on the radio the other day, the Third Programme it was too, and I could have contradicted him half a dozen times. And there was me, a head bursting with knowledge, and no one to pass it on to—except the Ficus elastica, and believe me, plant or not, it was more intelligent, more understanding, and a better companion than half a dozen people I could name." And he became silent again.

When we called to visit Sayed he was nowhere to
be seen. He wasn't in the side ward, he wasn't in
the big ward.

"I knew it," said Mrs. M. "I knew he wouldn't
last the night. Poor sod. But they might have called
us. They shouldn't have let him die alone." She
grabbed a passing nurse.

"What have you done with him?"

The nurse looked at her and looked at me, a
little frightened.

"What have you done with him? Sayed, the black
fellow who was in the corner here? Is he in the
morgue? Why didn't you call us?"

"The boy from Pakistan in the corner? Sayed?"

"That's him. What have you done with him?"

"He was moved this morning. His family came
to fetch him."

"His family?"

"His father. He arrived from Karachi last night,

156

and had him moved to the London Clinic this morning."

When we got back home there was a funeral-sized motor-car waiting by the door, and a dark-skinned man with a small black moustache leaning against it. He had come to collect the black fellow's belongings.

"He's not coming back then?" I said.

"No, I'm afraid not," he said.

"You'll apologize to him about my heater, won't you?'

"Your heater?"

"Yes, it was an accident you see. It was an old thing I had borrowed from a friend and it caught fire."

"I see."

"And will you give him regards—from Cyril, the fellow downstairs, he'll know what you mean."

"From Cyril?"

"The fellow downstairs."

"I'll certainly tell him."

And he saluted and was off.

"He must have been a maharajah," said Mrs. M. "He must have been with a car that size—and the London Clinic."

"The London Clinic?"

"Yes, that's where all the very rich go to die. There's some who spend more dying there than most people spend on living. Yes, I should have kept a visitor's book in my house. I had an Arab

Sheikh here once, a Polish count, two Irish gentlemen of ancient extraction—living together like man and wife—but nobody's been here any length of time who's left on his own two feet—except that rascal of a husband. Makes you think, doesn't it? Two of them died in bed. One fell down the stairs. One fell out of the window, and one jumped out. They were nearly all potty, but you get that with ancient blood."

"You can get potty with modern blood too," I said.

"Oh you can, and it's when you start mixing the ancient and modern that things get out of hand. What's wrong with the British working class is that it's been impregnated with upper-class blood."

"Impregnated?"

"Yes. You see nowadays when an aristocrat wants to sleep with his neighbor's wife, he can, the same as everybody else. But he couldn't a generation or two ago. If he wanted to commit adultery he had to commit it out of his class, the same with his wife, and that's how they impregnated the working class. The British working class has been corrupted by aristocratic blood."

"And where did the aristocrats get corrupted from?"

"They were born corrupt."

George called for me this morning earlier than usual.

"This is it," he said, "a perfect day, sunny, dry, with only a breath of wind. It's P-day."

"P-day?"

"Park day. March 7th this is: November, December, January, February, March. Five months almost to the day since we were in the park. I've almost forgotten what it looks like."

I got ready while he waited impatiently, almost jumping up and down with excitement.

We walked down the road, past the library, and on past the hospital, and then up the hill all the way to the park.

"It's quite a climb," said George. "I remember when I was a boy we used to go sledging down this hill in the winter. It was a grass-covered slope. I cracked my head against a tree almost where I'm standing now, and down there at the bottom near

159

the hospital, that used to be marsh, with moor hens paddling about in the reeds. Changed, hasn't it?"

From where we stood we had a view of black roof-tops and red houses as far as the eye could see, and here and there clumps of trees.

"There used to be trees in every street. Some are still there, but they hardly ever come into leaf. There's more abandoned cars now than anything else. They're using the street as a car cemetery."

We were now nearly at the top of the hill and were puffing heavily.

"You know," he said, "when the snow came I thought I had seen the park for the last time. I didn't think I was ever going to make it."

"We're not there yet," I said. The trouble in my leg had started to creep back. There wasn't a pain or anything like that, but while I moved on the leg kept staying in the same place, and I had to drag it behind like a bag of coals. But we made it, and we stood in the entrance, happy but still gasping.

We sat down and waited to draw breath before moving on to our usual spot by the flower beds. George couldn't wait to get up again.

"Can't we wait a bit yet?" I said, "there's hardly any flowers at this time of the year."

"Hardly any flowers in March? It'll be wild with daffodils, maybe even tulips. It'll be all over with the crocuses I suppose."

And he got to his feet and I puffed after him. We hadn't gone five yards when he suddenly stopped with his legs wide apart and his hand to his side, an odd position as if he was about to do a dance.

"Are you all right, George?"

He said nothing.

"George, are you all right?"

"Something's burst," he said, in a voice so quiet that I could hardly hear him. His face turned gray, and he sat down suddenly on the gravel path. A small crowd collected.

I bent down to pull him to the bench, but a park keeper told me not to move him and he rushed to call an ambulance. He was now lying flat on the ground with little pearls of perspiration forming on his forehead. I put my coat over him and somebody else put a coat beneath his head.

"You'll be all right in a jiffy, George. They're off for an ambulance. You'll be fine." He was breathing heavily, with his eyes shut.

"You'll be all right in a jiffy, George. The ambulance is on the way. Something like this happened about a year ago, do you remember? In the library it was. You were reading a paper and suddenly you threw it up in the air and dropped. I thought it was something you had seen in the headlines. And Dick, do you remember Dick? He was with us then and he thought you were over and done with. Remember. Well here you are hale and hearty—"

His breathing was now quieter and his jaw was opening and shutting like a fish.

161

The ambulance took about half an hour in coming and by then there was a large crowd round him. His nose and ears had turned black.

The ambulance men gave him oxygen, but he didn't stir.

"He's had a fair innings by the looks of him," said one of the men, and they almost flung him into the ambulance and drove off.

It was a small funeral, Mrs. McConnachie, Dora, and myself, and the same little parson who buried old Harry. George himself came in a small coffin, hardly bigger than a baby's bath, but in a huge hearse, and buried under a heap of flowers.

"It's a bit late in life to make a splash," said Mrs. M as we drove to the cemetery.

Dora didn't say anything. She was dressed in black and sobbing as if she had lost her own father. I thought she had just come for the ride.

"She likes funerals because she looks good in black," said Mrs. M.

And so she did, especially in her short, tight skirt. She had black stockings on too, and black lace to her petticoat. That was one mourner George couldn't have bargained for.

"Look at her snuffling away like a leaking tap," said Mrs. M. "I think there was something on between those two."

163

"I'm sorry for him," she said.

"Sorry for him? He was eighty-four. If I should ever get to that age I'll be sorry for myself."

"I'm that age," I said.

"Are you, Cyril?"

"I am."

"Eighty-four?"

"Last November."

"And I wouldn't have thought you were a day over eighty-three. Here, Dora—give over your snuffling will you—would you have thought Cyril here was eighty-four? A fine, healthy, well-preserved man like him?"

"Eighty-four? Never."

"And besides, it's different with men. A woman when she gets to our age is finished—"

"Speak for yourself," said Dora.

"—but men can go on for ever. Some men don't begin living till they're about seventy—that's about twenty years after most women have stopped."

"Speak for yourself," said Dora again, and we drove on in silence, except for Dora's sobbing. Then she said, "I think I'd like to be cremated."

"What, dear?" said Mrs. M.

"I'd like to be cremated."

"What? And make an ash of yourself?" Mrs. M thought that was very funny, but Dora didn't.

"Sorry, love," said Mrs. M. "I'm feeling in a comical mood. If you want to be cremated you go right ahead and be cremated. I think I'd like to be embalmed."

164

"Embalmed?" I said.

"Stuffed," she said.

"Like George's cat."

"I'd like to be embalmed and kept in a glass case on somebody's mantelpiece."

"It would have to be a bloody big case," said Dora, "and a bloody big mantelpiece."

"When you get embalmed," I said, "what do they stuff you with?"

"I don't know. Dora, you're the expert on stuffing. What do they stuff you with when you get embalmed?"

"Sage."

Mrs. M pulled me aside, and whispered, "She's in one of her moods."

The air in the cemetery was nippy and the little parson was waiting for us by the graveside stamping his feet and blowing his hands.

"Ah," he said, "there you are. I gathered it was one of you two gentlemen, but the deceased is the other one I take it. He was a fine little man—good things are always contained in small vessels. Fine little man. A Christian. I confess I never saw him in church, but there is more to Christianity than church-going. Had he lived longer he would, I am sure, have seen the light." And I looked down at George's coffin, half expecting him to get up and argue.

He was wheeled past a row of friends, Dick, Albert, Stephen, Ernie, Bill, all old soldiers like him, and their stones stood up like a guard of honor. There was Harry's grave too but without a stone: the soil had hardly settled on it.

The service was short, with Dora sobbing and seagulls screeching overhead, and we lowered his coffin till it came to rest with a thump on the gravelly bottom.

As I turned to go back to the car, my leg stopped where it was and I had to drag it behind me like a bag of coals.

I've been trying to work out why I'm not upset. I was very upset when old Harry went, and Dick, and I was closer to George than to either of them. But I don't feel upset at all. If anything I feel lighter, and younger, as if George was something dead and heavy which had been cut away from me. It could be the weather. It's been bright all day, with pale blue skies, and wisps of cloud across the arch like a line of white hair. I couldn't remember feeling chirpier. Of course George could be a nuisance. His grumbles, the way he looked, the way he spoke made him a wet blanket, and going out with him was like having a small piece of night tagging on to you. One day I would wake up and feel very sorry that I'd seen the last of him, but I wasn't sorry now I felt like a new man.

Mrs. M came up with a pot of tea and a plate of eggs and bacon to console me, but when she saw me up and about, whistling, and washing up my

cup and saucer, her mouth opened so wide that her
fag fell into the bacon and hissed there for ten
seconds before she knew what had happened.

"Are you all right?" she said.

"All right? Why shouldn't I be?"

"Don't know. Just asked. I brought you up a bite,
but you've eaten I see."

"I have."

And she went back down the stairs with her tea
and eggs and bacon, shaking her head.

I took out my best suit from the cupboard and
tried it on. It had been made during the war when
turn-ups weren't allowed, but from what I heard
they were making trousers without turn-ups again,
so it was fashionable enough. And it had kept its
shape. The trouble was I hadn't, and it was a strain
to get the right buttons into the right button-holes,
but I managed and I took a bus into town. It was
something I hadn't done since the Victory celebrations.

London had changed since then. There were
whole streets I couldn't recognize. There were
parts of Oxford Street and Tottenham Court Road
which used to be like a garden, with great big bright
flowers sprouting wild all over them, but they were
nearly all filled in, and there was more foreign
language spoken on top of the bus than English.
But I liked it, and the girls were very pretty, in very
short skirts, just like they used to have during the
war. Skirts and turn-ups seemed to have had their

ups and downs together. I had lunch in a Lyons tea shop—something else I hadn't done since the Victory celebrations—soup, pie and chips, trifle and tea. Nearly six bob it cost me altogether. I wonder what George would have said to that.

I wasn't used to slap-up meals like that, four courses, one piled on top of the other, and then I went on to a News Cinema. I fell asleep almost as soon as I sat down. I woke about a couple of hours later and remained to see the show five or six times. It was more enjoyable the first time than the sixth time, but it had only cost me a bob to get in so I got my money's worth. It would have cost me more than that to keep warm back home.

And it wasn't only the films. I liked the company, At first it was all great big women, crushing past me, piled high with shopping bags and parcels, and schoolboys, rolling their own cigarettes, smoking and swearing. Later it was young couples, fellows with pretty young girls, who didn't seem at all interested in what was happening on the screen. By the time it was all over I was about the only one sitting upright.

I woke this morning bursting with cheer. Bits of it kept seeping out during the day, and a lot seeped out while I was in the pictures. By the time I got back it had all escaped, and I felt very tired and very sad.

I stood outside the house for a long time. There was no light upstairs where the black fellow used to

169

work and none downstairs where Mrs. M lived. I should have left the light on in my own room to welcome me back. I walked up the black and white diamond shaped tiles to the door, and then walked back. I don't know if I was afraid to go in, or what, but I certainly did not want to go in. It must have been very late for the traffic had nearly all died down, and the lights were popping out in the upstairs windows all along the street. It was windy and scraps of paper and dead leaves bounced along the road and swirled round my legs.

As I was standing there I suddenly heard a cackle, almost like a burst of gun-fire, and a minute later Mrs. McConnachie came staggering round the corner, arm in arm with a man I had never seen before.

When she saw me by the gate she stood swaying there for a minute, as if doubting it was me.

"Shrill," she said, "what you doing out of bed at this time of the night?"

"I was just having a walk."

"Ish having a walk," she explained to her friend. He was a podgy, red-faced man with sleek hair and a scar under one eye.

"This gentleman," she said, "has come to fix me up with an immersion-heater," and she cackled so loudly that the lights came on again all along the street. She quietened down, and they went on tip-toe, up the path and into the house, she with her arm around his waist and he with a hand on her buttock.

I was wakened by the door bell. It was Dora.

"I'll be down in a minute," I shouted, and switched on the wireless, slapped water over my face and put my greatcoat over my pajamas. It sounded like Music While You Work, which meant that it was nearly eleven o'clock. I had slept in badly.

Dora looked me up and down, my greatcoat, my pajamas and my galoshes.

"Have you been ill?" she said.

"No."

"Are you just out of bed?"

"Yes, I slept in badly . . ."

"I'll say you have, it's ten to four."

"It can't be."

She put her wrist under my nose. "Here, see for yourself."

"My God."

"And I suppose she's slept in as well."

"She?"

"Flora."

"I don't know."

"She was supposed to have called for me at half past two and didn't. Is she in?"

"I really don't know."

She came in after me and we tried the kitchen door. It was locked.

"This isn't like Flora. You've no idea where she is?"

"No."

And she stood by the door for a while before walking off with a rapid clip-clap of high heels.

I had hardly made my bed when the door bell went again. I nipped over to the window to see who it was and nearly dropped. It could have been George. A small man, in a large black coat, with a cloth cap and a walking stick. I was still in my great-coat, pajamas, and galoshes, so he looked me up and down the same as Dora.

"You're not Mrs. McConnachie then?" he said.

"She's out."

"Out you said?"

"She's out."

"She's not in then?"

"No."

"It's the room, you see. I've come about the room."

"The room?"

"Yes, you see it's the card she has in the shop. I don't suppose you'll know how much she wants?"

"No."

"It'll be too much, it always is. They're wanting more for rooms now than they used to want for houses. When I got married you could pay twenty-five pounds down, and that was you with a house—not that I had twenty-five pounds. But twenty-five pounds down, and that was you with a house. Now they're asking you two pounds a week for a room. Now there's fifty-two weeks in the year—at least there was when I was a young man, I suppose that's gone up with everything else. Everything goes up, except the size of rooms, they go down, and my blood pressure, that's been going down too. You'd think if high blood pressure was bad, then low blood pressure would be good, but it doesn't work that way at all. It was high blood pressure that killed her and it looks as if low blood pressure'll kill me. Yes. I suppose if I had had my low blood pressure about the same time as she had her high we might have been able to swop bits of blood and level things out, at least that's what I said to the doctor, but he said things don't work that way. Nothing seems to work the way it should.

"Well, on account of me being an invalid, she was the breadwinner, and when she died it was a very great shock to me. We had a nice house, and I had to move from that, then it was to two rooms and kitchen, then a room and kitchen, and for the last three or four years it's been rooms. It's funny how when you get a really small room you'd think rooms couldn't possibly get smaller, but they do, you know, they do all the time, and they got smaller every time I moved. The room I have now is just about the size of my bed. In fact I've got to clamber over the bed to get into it. It would have been all right, only I had a difference with my landlady. She said I used the lavatory at awkward times. I said it wasn't me who works out the times I have to use the lavatory. She said she can't help that. I said I couldn't help it either. If you've got to go, you've got to go. She said my pulling the lavatory chain in the early hours of the morning woke up the whole house. So I had an idea and stopped pulling the chain, but that didn't please her either, and now she's asked me to go. I don't mind moving much. It always makes a change, and you get to know new people, but it's the expense. There's a man with a van and I'm his regular customer, but it's fifteen bob a time, and fifteen bob is money. I remember the time when for fifteen bob—"

All the time he was speaking I was moving from one leg to the other because I wanted to go to the toilet. Also I wasn't dressed yet and it was nippy. I tried to explain that Mrs. M wasn't in and that I had no idea when she would be back, but I couldn't get a word in edgeways, and finally I did the only thing I could do, and slammed the door in his face. And even that didn't shut him up, for I could hear his voice going as I was racing up the stairs.

Dora called again in the evening. "She hasn't been back?"

"No."

"And she hasn't phoned?"

"No."

"I'm going to the police."

"She'll be back," I said. "She's been away for weeks before."

"Not without me knowing about it. This is unlike her. When did you last see her?"

"Last night."

"Before she went out?"

"No, when she came back."

"Was she with a fellow?"

"With a fellow?"

"She was, wasn't she. A fat, horrible-looking type, with sleek hair and a scar?"

"Yes."

"God forgive us. We do terrible things when we're lonely. It was somebody she picked up in the pub. Did they leave together?"

"No, that's the last I saw of them."

"You didn't hear any coming or going after that?"

"No. I was very tired and fell asleep as soon as I got into bed."

"I'm worried, I'm very worried."

"What could have happened to her?"

"I'm afraid to think. She hasn't phoned or anything?"

"No."

"I'm going to the police."

About an hour later a police car pulled up and

175

questioned me for over an hour about Mrs. M, her movements, her private life, what she did, who she went with. I couldn't help them much. They took down everything I said, and tried the handle of the kitchen door.

"You haven't a key for it?"

"No," I said, "that's her private part."

And they left. They came back five minutes later to rummage around the top floor, tried the handle of the kitchen door, and drove off again.

I hadn't dressed yet when the door bell went. I rushed down hurriedly thinking it was Dora. It was the little old man of yesterday.

"I've come about the—" he began, and I slammed the door in his face before he could finish.

I hardly got back to my room when the bell went again. I went down again, this time, slowly, getting ready to give him a mouthful. But it wasn't him. It was the black fellow, Sayed, leaning on a walking stick, and smiling.

"Ah, it's you," I said. "So you're all right?"

"Not perfect. I'm better. And how are you all?"

"Very well, very well. Yes, we're fine."

"And your small friend, how do you call him?"

"George? He's very well too. He's dead."

"Dead? I'm sorry to hear it. Will you give him my condolences?"

"Yes, I will, the next time I see him."

"And is the good lady of the establishment in?"

"The good lady of the establishment?"

"Our dear Mrs. McConnachie."

"She's vanished."

And as we were talking a whole line of police cars pulled up. Dora was with them looking white and tear-stained.

They didn't seem to want anything more from me, so we went upstairs to keep out of the way. I was filling the kettle when suddenly there was a piercing scream. I dropped the kettle on my toe, but hardly felt it. The black fellow sat on the bed as if he was nailed there, grasping the cover tightly. A minute later a policeman came up.

"You had better come with us," he said.

By the time I got dressed the road was jammed with cars, and a crowd six-deep hemmed in against the houses on the other side. They gave me a small cheer when I came out as if I was some sort of hero and they crowded round the police car. The last person I could see as we drove away was the little old man, George II, waving me good-bye.

It was a large car, funeral size, and if it wasn't for the speed we could have been going to a burial.

In the police station I was left by a large wooden table in an empty room with a police sergeant scribbling busily at a high desk beside me. Telephones kept ringing, people came and went, but no one had anything to say to me. I cleared my throat several times and coughed to show I was there but they still ignored me, and after a time I began to doubt if I really was there. Perhaps I had snuffed it. That scribbling police sergeant with the spectacles could have been the Recording Angel, and this place with the table could have been the waiting-room to wherever I was going. I was here to be vetted. It all seemed very likely. The only unlikely part of it was the ringing telephones, and the policemen coming and going in a constant rush. It was the rush which spoilt things.

I must have been there for an hour or two when the Recording Angel police sergeant looked over his glasses and said, "Would you like to leave the room or something?"

"Would I like to leave the room?"

"Yes."

"I would like to get back home if that's all right with you."

"You can't do that for a minute yet, but you wouldn't like to leave the room?"

"No."

So he got off his high chair, opened a window and got back to his scribbling.

I was beginning to get tired of crossing my legs and uncrossing them, getting up and sitting down, when a young man in plain clothes came in.

"We've got him," he said to the sergeant. "Found him in bed with a bird, that's the last bird he'll be bedding for a while."

"He'll stretch I suppose," said the sergeant, continuing to scribble.

"And how. Murder in the course of robbery. He rifled the old girl's handbag."

The sergeant shook his head sadly.

"There was a time," he said, "when people were satisfied with a bit of honest adultery, but not now."

And he returned to his scribbling with a sigh.

The little parson greeted us with a cheer.

"Here we are again," he said merrily. "We've been seeing a lot of each other lately, haven't we?"

There were three of us at the funeral: Dora, the black fellow, and myself. As the parson was beginning the service we heard running footsteps on the gravel, and a thin, bald-headed man joined us. Dora seemed to know him, for she took one glance at him, and quickly looked away. I had seen him before, and while the parson went on, I tried to think where.

Mrs. M was quite a weight, poor dear, and as we lowered her into the grave, she nearly pulled us with her, and the parson slipped and went clattering down on top of the coffin.

"All a little prematurely," he said as we hauled him out.

When we got back home I was turning the key in the door when I suddenly pulled back. There was someone inside.

181

"It must be your imagination," said the black fellow. "I am away. You are away. Poor Mrs. Mc-Connachie has departed, there can be no one inside."

"Listen."

We listened. There were footsteps on the stairs.

The black fellow turned to run, and I followed, but a voice called us back.

It was the man we had seen in the cemetery. He was standing by the door in a waistcoat and shirt sleeves.

"What did you want?" he said.

"This gentleman lives here," said the black fellow, "and I was seeing him. I used to live here."

Now I remembered who he was. He had called for Mrs. McConnachie that evening I was in by myself.

"Well I'm the new landlord," he said. "I'm Mr. McConnachie."

"Ah, my condolences," said the black fellow. "She was a very fine woman."

"Very helpful," I said, "very kind."

"Well, you can piss off, the pair of you," he said. "I'm having no blacks here, and no bed-wetting old buggers either."

I woke early this morning and I was out and about
looking for a room before the town had come to
life. Every house in the district seemed to have a
room to let, but they all wanted fancy prices, two
pounds, three pounds, even four. Four pounds for
a room! I didn't think people paid that much for
a house. But after searching round for half the
morning I did find one room which was twenty-
nine shillings and sixpence.

The lady who opened the door was tall, and
thin, and very neat-looking, with gray hair that sat
on her head like a helmet.

She looked me up and down and then length-
wise and breadthwise and she asked me to follow
her upstairs.

"I should warn you that it is not a very large
room," she said, pushing the door hard against the
bed so that I could squeeze through, "on the other
hand it is extremely economic on fuel, and of
course, it is very easy to keep clean. It has one

further advantage. You have access to almost every part of the room without moving from the bed. Everything is almost within arm's reach—which is a great boon to the bed-ridden and elderly, don't you think? And it is all so cozy. And as I said it is extremely, but extremely economic on fuel. As a matter of fact some of my previous tenants found that they could keep themselves warm in winter merely by being in the room. But before we go any further I hope you will permit me to ask you a question or two. Do you keep livestock?"

"Livestock?"

"Pets. Dogs, cats, hamsters, white mice, budgerigars?"

"No."

"I'm so glad. Livestock is inclined to be messy, and this is a house-proud house. I don't mind plants. That potted fern on the window sill goes with the room. It is provided at no extra charge, but I do have a certain antipathy to rubber-plants. They do tend to get a little out of hand. Now I hope you don't mind if I ask you one or two rather more delicate questions." She paused for a moment. "Are you in the habit of bringing women up to your room? One tries to be broad-minded about these things, but it is a single room. If you wanted a double room it would be a different matter."

"No, I don't bring women home."

"Splendid. And are you—how does one put it?—are you continent?"

"Am I what?"

"Continent."

"No. English born and bred."

"Yes, that is a blessing, so very few people are. But I don't think you quite grasped my question. Are you in full command of your bowels and bladder?"

"My bowels and bladder?"

"What I mean is, do they function when you want them to function, or are they of an independent disposition?"

"I haven't thought about it. I suppose they function when I want them to function."

"You suppose?"

"I don't leak if that's what you mean."

"Yes, that's what I did mean. Excellent. There remains only one other question. Are you in the habit of using the toilet in the early hours of the morning?"

"Am I?"

"Do you use the toilet between midnight and seven A.M.?"

"I don't know, I don't have a watch, but I do have to get up in the night every now and again."

"Every now and again, but not every night?"

"No, not every night."

"But you do some nights?"

"Winter nights mostly."

"We do supply our tenants with decorated chamber pots for minor use."

185

"Don't use them," I said, "never have done, never shall."

And that was the end of that.

I tried the two pound rooms and didn't have much luck there either. No one wants small children, dogs, or old men with stomach conditions— not that I have a condition, but they all felt that at my age I was what one lady called "a condition suspect."

I was already on the way to see what the Salvation Army had to offer when I bumped into Dora.

"You're looking for a room?" she said. "Why didn't you come to me, you know I let rooms."

"I heard they were expensive."

"Where did you hear that from?"

"Well, all rooms are."

"How much can you afford to pay?"

"How much can I afford to pay?"

"How much rent can you afford?"

"I suppose I could scratch up fifteen shillings— a pound."

"You can't get a room for that, Cyril. Flora must have been robbing herself if she charged you that."

"Twenty-five shillings," I said.

"Can you afford thirty?"

"Thirty shillings a week?"

"Yes."

"I suppose I could, with a pinch."

It took me nearly an hour to get to the park because my new room is farther from it than the old one and because my leg has been playing me up again. It was a bright day, but windy and cold and I had my greatcoat on and came with a stick in hand.

It's a week now since George died and I only began to miss him last night, just after I moved into my new room. I had everything in place, the wireless on, the kettle on the boil, a bun all buttered for eating, when suddenly I felt very sad, very lonely, and a little frightened, as if all I had left had been frozen up in a lump of black ice and suddenly melted. I couldn't even eat the bun and drink the tea, and the wireless became a noise.

I went out into the hall, but there was nobody to talk to. It was a large building full of rooms, and the rooms were full of people. You could hear their radios, and smell their soup, but you never saw anyone.

187

I put on my coat and went out for a walk down the road to where I had lived before. The house was in darkness with a lot of empty milk bottles on the doorstep and a pane in the downstairs window broken. There were weeds sprouting between the diamond-shaped tiles on the path. They must have been there before, only I just noticed them now. They shivered in the wind.

Two or three weeks ago this had been the happiest house in the street, with the black fellow busy upstairs, with all his books and papers, and Mrs. M cackling away downstairs, and me in the middle with my friends coming and going. Now the black fellow was gone, and I was gone, and poor Mrs. M had her head bashed in—which was even worse than dying. Dying, at least, is respectable. I looked at the house now, big, black, sad, and empty. It was exactly how I felt.

When I got back to my place there was a woman going up the stairs with a man holding up her backside as if it might fall off. I said good evening to them, but they didn't even turn round, and hurried on ahead of me.

I felt better when I woke this morning. As I've always said, if you can sleep you can't complain about anything and that's one thing I can do, I can sleep. I may be woken by this or that several times in the night, but I drop back to sleep as soon as my head touches the pillow.

I was a bit nervous about the park, because since

last November something had always cropped up to stop me; first the rain, then the snow, then the fog. Then, when we finally reached it, poor George dropped dead. Now, as I got nearer, I was afraid I might do the same. In fact when I got to the entrance I took off my cap and stood there bareheaded, almost defying whoever was responsible to have a go. But nothing happened. I put my cap back on, thinking that perhaps I might live forever.

As I walked on I again had that odd feeling which I get on and off now, that I was dead and the park was the Garden of Eden, for there wasn't a soul about. No old men, no young mothers pushing prams, no stout ladies walking dogs, no long-haired men in sandals sketching daffodils, no schoolboys playing truant, not even park keepers. There was not a soul to be seen, not a soul to be heard.

And suddenly it began to rain, at first lightly and then heavily. I looked around for shelter. There was only the old men's hut.

George used to warn me about using that hut. "Old age is contagious," he used to say, but I reckoned old age was better than pneumonia and I ran without stopping.

There was only one man there, small, with a white face and in a big black coat. If I hadn't seen him before I would have been sure it was the reincarnation of George.

"It's yourself," he said as soon as I came in.

"Yes. Wet, isn't it? It didn't look like wet this morning, but it is now."

He looked me over. "Do you come here often?"

"No."

"I used to, every day, but I haven't been since November. I used to meet all my friends, see. But they're not here today. They're not likely to be here tomorrow either. They're dead, you see. This has been a bad winter."

"It has."

"I lost two of my friends only last month, and my mother the month before that, and my pension book the week after, and other things all over the place. What's your name?"

"Cyril."

"Mine is Agamemnon. It's an odd name that. I got it from my father. His family was full of odd names. He had a brother called Hercules who was even smaller than me. It's all right having a name like Agamemnon if you're called Agamemnon. But I've had to go through life being called Ugh. You can call me Ugh if you like."

"Ugh?"

"Ugh."

"My name is Cyril."

"Cyril?"

"Yes."

"I had an aunt called Hecuba, and she used to be known as Heck. We had two Hecks in the family. There was the Heck for Hecuba, and the Heck

190

for Hector, and, although one was an uncle and the other an aunt, you couldn't always be sure which was which. My wife's name was Victoria, after the Queen you see. They weren't related, but all her sisters were called after queens and all her brothers after kings. She had high blood pressure, my wife did. I had low blood pressure. I still have, though I suppose at my age I'm lucky having any blood at all. How are you off for blood?"

"Blood?"

"Yes."

"I've enough to get on with."

"It's a funny thing, blood. I read in the Reader's Digest . . ."

The rain came down heavily and rapped on the roof like machine-gun-fire.